A Jacana book

The Serpent Under

Rob Marsh

First published in 2003 by **Jacana Media (Pty) Ltd**
5 St Peter Rd
Houghton
2041
South Africa

ISBN 1-919931-48-1

Cover design by **Disturbance**
disturb@mweb.co.za

Printed by **Fishwicks**
Durban

See a complete list of Jacana titles at www.jacana.co.za

To Janette
with love

"Look like the innocent flower
But be the serpent under't."

 Macbeth 1.V.61

Contents

MATTHEW'S STORY

ONE

BEFORE I MET BRENDA I didn't know that killing a person could be so easy. I'm not talking about killing someone by mistake, accidentally tripping them up on the stairs or knocking them over with a car, that sort of thing. I mean actual murder, with malice, forethought and in cold blood. Take my word, it's a lot simpler than most people think.

I know there are those who will say I'm a monster because of what I've done, but I didn't set out to hurt anyone. In fact, a lot of things that happened occurred by accident almost. That's why I've decided to explain, to give my side of the story and to put things into perspective, I mean.

I think I should start out by saying that I believe I'm more determined and ambitious than most people. This is important because when you're determined and ambitious, individuals sometimes get in your way and you have to take them out of the game, so to speak. That doesn't always mean killing them, of course. I'm not advocating violence as a means to an end, I'm just saying that there are times when violence can be the only practical and effective method one has of obtaining a specific goal. And we all have goals that we want to achieve, don't we?

I'd been working in the Finance Department at Thompsons Manufacturing for five years when Brenda joined the firm as a secretary. I remember watching Mrs Williams, the head of Personnel, show her to her desk. After she'd introduced Brenda to the other typists, she handed her over to Jenny Martin, the head of Secretarial and then ran back to her office in the Administration Building. Secretarial, by the way, is the word management uses when they mean the typing pool. All the typists in Secretarial share a big, open-plan office on the top floor of the Production Building, which is just another name for the factory.

My office was also on the Secretarial floor, but was at the far end, away from everyone else. I've never liked Mrs Williams because she's always struck me as being stuck-up and too full of her own self-importance. For example, take the time I ended up sitting next to her in the canteen during a staff meeting. Just to make conversation I started telling her about my plans for the future. She suddenly interrupted, saying: "It's not always a good idea to be too ambitious, Matthew," which, in my opinion, was an uncalled for thing to say. I think she thought I was getting "above my station", if you know what I mean. Either that or she was just plain jealous because she knew that I was capable of great things.

She's also always dressed up to the nines, like mutton dressed up as lamb, as my Aunt Sal would have said. And she's very fond of putting on airs and graces – as if having an office in the Administration Building somehow meant that she was better than the rest of us.

A couple of times when I'd been over to Administration, I'd caught her in her office holding up a little gold compact and staring at her face in the mirror. One time she was putting on lipstick, and another she was dabbing face powder on her cheeks, but the moment she saw me she quickly put her make-up away, acting like she'd finished what she was doing anyway. But then they all behave like that, the bosses, I mean, pretending to be "part of the team" one minute and playing the lord high and mighty the next. It's like they think that the rest of us are stupid and don't know what they're up to.

It may sound strange but I knew Brenda was special the first time I laid eyes on her. That's why I immediately made a note about her in my desk diary. The note said: GP started today. I didn't know her name then, but what struck me about her were her dark eyes and long, black hair. GP stood for Gypsy Princess.

I think it's necessary to explain that I'd always made a point of maintaining the correct professional distance where the typists are concerned. That's why I didn't go and introduce myself, because I didn't want to appear forward, and is the reason I didn't actually get to speak to her until she'd been working at the firm for almost a week.

From my first day at Thompsons, I'd always made an effort to keep myself to myself. That was to prevent any kind of salacious gossip, particularly as I knew one or two of the girls had something of a reputation with men, if you know what I mean. It was also true to say that until Brenda arrived none of the other girls had ever held any interest for me. They were a common, empty-headed bunch, in my opinion. Men seemed to be their main topic of conversation, except for the married ones that is, who only talked about babies.

My office wasn't really an office, by the way, at least not in the normal sense of the word, it was more a small open booth or cubicle. There were five of these cubicles in a line along the far wall of the Secretarial floor. Put together, they looked like a row of horse stalls, which was the name most people used when they were talking about my part of the building.

My "office" was the centre cubicle and the only one still being used. It contained a desk; a chair and two grey filing cabinets that were pushed up against the back wall. In one filing cabinet I kept all the payroll files for the company, all listed in alphabetical order and in the other, everyone's personal and banking details. Over the desk was a neon strip light hanging on a long chain from one of the roof girders.

All the other cubicles had become dumping grounds and were full of rubbish. When I first joined the firm I wrote some memos to Mr Goodison, the managing director, asking that something be done about this "unacceptable waste of space", as I called it, but even though I eventually got a reply from his secretary saying the matter would be looked into, nothing happened, so in the end I gave up trying.

My job was to keep track of salary payments and to record any absenteeism that occurred, including sick or annual leave. All this information I kept on computer, of course, but Dick Butler, the finance director, a complete moron who couldn't tell a computer from a combine harvester, insisted on a paper backup too, which is why I was always having to shuffle through the files and send him a "hard copy" every time he had any sort of query to deal with.

Anyway, the first time I spoke to Brenda was when she brought me a letter to sign. I was writing in a ledger and hadn't noticed her come in to my office. When I finally looked up she was standing right in front of my desk, staring down. I asked her how long she'd been standing there.

I spoke sharply because I wanted her to realise right from the start that I wasn't to be trifled with. Instead of answering, she just shrugged and pushed a strand of hair back behind her ear, which is a habit she has. The strange thing was she never once took her eyes off me, or even blinked, which was slightly disconcerting, to tell you the truth.

"Jenny told me to get you to sign this," she said after a long pause.

I took the letter, put my signature on the bottom without reading it and threw it back at her.

"Thank you," she said and went back to her desk.

I suppose it was what you'd call a brief encounter, but it made an impression on me because I felt like I'd been assessed in some way. I don't like being subject to such close scrutiny, which is half the reason I was so off-hand with her.

Brenda is very striking to look at, by the way. Most people would agree that she's very attractive, what with her big green eyes and long black hair, but she's hardly what you'd call your classic English rose. Even though she's tall and thin with a "model stature", as I once heard Jenny Martin call it, she dresses differently to most girls. You'll never see Brenda in jeans or a T-shirt, for example. Mostly she wears long swirly cotton dresses that she gets from an Indian shop in the high street. She's also very fond of black eyeliner and that makes her look quite foreign, Middle Eastern, I suppose, even though she's English, born and bred. That's why I called her the Gypsy Princess before I knew her name, because she looked so foreign, I mean.

Sometimes, when I didn't have a lot to do, I'd pretend to work on a file on my desk so that I could watch her out of the corner of my eye. She had a very graceful way of moving and I got the impression that she was a very quiet, serene sort of person, someone who did yoga or meditation, that kind of thing. I also thought she was probably quite innocent, naïve almost, which is a quality I find quite appealing, especially nowadays, when most of the girls I come into contact with seem to be so sure of themselves. I want to say though, that even when I used to spy on her, I wasn't doing it with the intention of starting up a relationship or anything like that, I was just interested because she seemed so different to all the other typists.

After our first, brief conversation, the next time I really spoke to her was about a week later. She came into my office just when lunch break was ending.

"Why don't you ever eat in the canteen with the rest of us?" she asked.

That day, she was wearing a long green and white cotton dress, a green headband and brown leather sandals, which made her look like a hippie. It was on the tip of my tongue to ask her what business it was of hers, but in the end I just said that I didn't want to.

After that I went back to the book I was reading. When she didn't move away, I looked up at her again, only more sternly the second time so that she could see how annoyed I was.

She gave me a funny look, more of a frown than anything else, looked like she was about to say something, then turned and walked away without a word. A minute later I saw her talking to one of the other secretaries in the typing pool. Stupid girl, I thought, but didn't think any more about it.

It was an hour later that Gloria, the girl Brenda had been talking to, banged a file down on my desk.

"Why were you so rude to Brenda today?" she said.

I knew who she was talking about, but decided to play dumb for a while.

"Who's Brenda?" I said.

"The new girl."

I said, "Oh, her," like the whole thing was totally unimportant.

"Well?"

I ignored the question, gave her a long bored look and then went back to the work I was doing.

"Well? Haven't you got anything to say?" she asked, all irritated now.

The last thing I wanted was a pointless argument. I had more important things to think about.

"No, I haven't, Gloria," I said.

"She was only trying to be friendly."

This time I shrugged instead of answering. That was when she finally got the message: that I wasn't interested and wasn't going to talk about it.

"You really get on my nerves," she said and stormed off to her desk.

13

I thought that would be the end of it, but the next day, Gloria was back in my office again, only this time she was all sweetness and light. When I didn't pay her much attention, she picked up the book I'd brought to work with me that morning. She suddenly looked all confused and I saw her lips move as she read the title.

"What's this you're reading, Matthew?" she asked.

I said that it was called *Also Sprach Zarathustra* by Friedrich Nietzsche. I nearly added, perhaps you'd like to borrow it for a day or two, Gloria, but thought the sarcasm would be wasted on her.

She read the title again, then put the book back down on my desk, but a lot quicker than she'd picked it up. You'd almost have thought it was going to burn her fingers or something. It was all I could do not to laugh.

"Never heard of it," she said.

I told her who Nietzsche was, that he was a philosopher who lived in the nineteenth century. "He created the concept of the *Übermensch* or Superman to justify the existence of the human race," I said.

I knew from the look on her face that she hadn't the faintest idea what I was talking about.

"You mean Superman from the films?"

She thought I was talking about the comic book character.

"No," I said, "another superman." Then I gave her a long explanation about Nietzsche's theories. "His Superman wasn't a product of long evolution," I said, "but someone of superior potential who emerges after he completely masters himself and strikes off conventional Christian herd morality in order to create his own values."

That made her even more baffled, if that was possible. Not that I was surprised, of course. For the girls in Secretarial, fine literature is something with "Mills & Boon" on the cover.

"Why can't you be nice to Brenda?" she said, changing the subject.

"I was nice to her," I said.

"You weren't very nice to her yesterday."

I said that I didn't know what she meant.

"She came to speak to you, but you ignored her."

"She wanted to know why I didn't eat in the canteen. I told her."

"She was just trying to be friendly."

"Yes, and I was friendly too."

That was when she gave me a look. "You're not a queer are you?" she said.

What a cow I thought, but I didn't let her see how angry I was just then. "No, I'm not a queer", I said as quietly and calmly as I could. "I'm just not that interested in your little friend Brenda."

She had to think about that for a few seconds. In the end she shrugged. "Please yourself then," she said. At that point she turned on her heel and walked back to her desk.

Two

For about two weeks after that I didn't have much to do with Brenda. We'd see each other every day at work, of course and sometimes she'd bring me an invoice to check or a letter to sign, but nothing happened that was out of the ordinary, if you know what I mean.

By the way, I think I should point out that even though I made an exception in Brenda's case, I still have a strict rule about never getting involved with a work colleague, no matter how appealing they might seem. In my opinion, one should always avoid emotional relationships at work, because affairs of the heart and affairs of the head simply don't mix. The case of Mr Ratcliffe, one of the directors, is a perfect example of what I mean.

When I first started at Thompsons it was common knowledge that Mr Ratcliffe was having it off with one of the secretaries. Apparently, they'd meet at a hotel once a week and it was rumoured they even went away for a dirty weekend together. It was all rather sordid, really. Anyway, after a time, his wife found out. One day she came to work and caused a terrible fuss, shouting and throwing things about in his office until in the end she had to be escorted off the premises by security. Of course, he resigned not long after that, even though he didn't have a job to go to and now he's divorced and living alone and on unemployment benefit. Sometimes I see him at the library, though we never acknowledge one another. He always looks very shabby and down in the mouth, which is nothing like he was when he was at work. I don't know what happened to the secretary. I gather that the affair ended not long after Mr Ratcliffe's wife threw a tantrum. Not surprisingly, the secretary left the firm shortly after he did. Someone told me she'd moved to another town, but I don't know if that's true.

Not everyone sees things the same way as I do, of course. The men from the factory are always finding excuses to come into the typing pool to chat to one or other of the girls, for example. Personally, I can't see what the attraction is. Most of the girls are very common and they're always telling each other what they got up to the night before, even the intimate details sometimes. At one time, two of the worst culprits developed the habit of standing outside my office talking in a loud voice about the disgusting things they'd done with their boyfriends, even though they knew very well that I could hear. I put up with them for a couple of days then I told them to go away and that I didn't want to hear such vulgarity, but they just giggled and carried on talking like I didn't exist. In the end I had to complain to Jenny Martin and threaten to go to Mrs Williams to make them stop.

I must confess that I don't have a great deal of experience where girls are concerned, not compared with some of the men I know who claim to have a different girlfriend every night, that is. I've had girlfriends, of course, but most of my relationships have been platonic. I have to say though that in my experience, most girls tend to be frivolous and silly and seem to lack any serious interests in life. All they want to do is to get married and settle down. Personally, I've always wanted to achieve great things, which is why I think there's much more to living than simply striving for a life of domestic bliss, which in my opinion, doesn't exist anyway. I don't want to give the impression that I don't know about the physical side of things, because that isn't true. I once hired a blue movie from a video shop, which proves I'm not a prude or anything like that, though I must confess that I found the whole thing rather distasteful.

Anyway, it wasn't until about a month after Brenda had started at Thompsons that it really dawned on me just how different she was compared to all the other girls.

I suppose the penny finally dropped when she came into my office one day to return a file she had been working on. It was during my tea break and I had my head buried in a book – as usual – so I didn't pay much attention to her until she asked me what I was reading.

The book was a translation of *Les 120 Journées de Sodome* by the Marquis de Sade, so at first I didn't want to answer. I thought she might have heard of de Sade and get the wrong idea, you see. If that happened in all likelihood she'd go around telling everyone in the building that I was a pervert who liked reading dirty books, which isn't true. Even now I don't really know what made me say what I did. Mostly, I suppose, it was because I was irritated at being interrupted and I thought the sooner I answered her, the sooner she'd go away.

"It's a book called *One Hundred and Twenty Days of Sodom* by the Marquis de Sade," I said.

After a pause, she said, "Isn't a Marquis a person who's rich or royal or something like that?"

I knew from the way that she'd answered that she'd never heard of de Sade, which didn't surprise me in the slightest.

I told her that de Sade was a Marquis, which is what people in this country would call a lord and that he lived around the time of the French Revolution, about two hundred years ago. I added that his family was related to one of the French royal houses and his father was a diplomat.

There was another pause, longer this time than the first one.

"What's it about? Your book, I mean," she said.

I could have lied to her, of course. I could have made up some innocent story and she wouldn't have been any the wiser, but there was something about the way she had asked the question that made me think she was genuinely interested, so I decided to shock her with the truth instead.

"It's about sex," I said.

I half expected her to snigger or make some kind of stupid comment, but she didn't say anything, she just nodded.

"De Sade was sent to prison for sexually abusing a prostitute," I continued. "He wrote *One Hundred and Twenty Days of Sodom* while he was locked away."

I thought she might cause a scene when I went into detail, but she just looked very thoughtful again. I think what amazed me most was how calm she was. All the other girls would have started giggling and performing the moment they heard the word "sex".

"Do you mean it's like the Kama Sutra?" she asked.

That was when I realised she was quite well read.

"No," I said. "The Kama Sutra is a kind of textbook about eroticism

18

and other forms of human pleasure. *One Hundred and Twenty Days of Sodom* is more like a personal diary."

Even though I could hear myself speaking, I couldn't actually believe I was saying such things. That's when I explained that although de Sade wrote about sex and personally did all the things he wrote about, some people think his books are more about ideas than sex.

She gave me the same funny look again. I couldn't make out what she was thinking.

"What kind of ideas?"

"About relationships," I said.

She stared at me. "I still don't understand what you mean."

I said that de Sade argued that it was right and proper for some people to do what they wanted to other people, even if it meant breaking the law.

"Is that what you think? That it's alright to do what you want to someone else, I mean?"

That was an interesting question, but I didn't know whether I should answer, not honestly, anyway. I did in the end, though.

"Yes," I said, when one person is superior to another, the superior person has the right to bend the inferior person to his or her will.

I could see that she wasn't convinced.

"What about if the inferior person gets hurt in the process?" she asked.

"That isn't the point," I said, a remark that seemed to throw her off her stride a bit.

"It is if you're getting knocked black and blue," she answered after she'd thought about it for a moment.

"The real question," I said, "is does one individual have the right to dominate and control another individual?"

That was when she wanted to know what I thought. I told her that I thought it was acceptable if the dominant person was superior.

"Superior as in stronger?"

"No, not physically superior, intellectually and emotionally superior."

I remember thinking that this was the first intelligent conversation I'd had at Thompsons. I thought she was going to ask me to explain what I meant again, but this time she just stood very still for a moment with her eyes closed. Eventually, she said very seriously, "But it's not possible for everyone to do what they want."

I agreed with her.

"But you're still saying that it's sometimes okay to do what you want to someone else, even if that someone else doesn't like it?"

She had spoken very coldly, like she had suddenly decided that she didn't like what she was hearing, but I'd already gone too far to turn back.

"Not exactly,' I said. "I'm saying that at times a superior person has the right to exercise power over an inferior person."

"Just because they're superior, as you call it?"

"Yes."

"I don't think that's right," she said, then turned and walked out of my office, without saying another word.

THREE

I WASN'T ALL THAT SURPRISED when I didn't see much of Brenda for a while after that. When we did meet at work, she didn't mention de Sade to me, nor did she tell any of the other girls what we'd been talking about, as far as I know. It was like we'd gone back to being strangers again. Not that I was bothered, mind you, because I had other things on my mind: I had applied for the job of senior clerk, but had been turned down, you see.

The position had originally been advertised on the staff notice board and I'd applied straight away. Mrs Williams had called me for an interview the day after my application went in, but that was just for show. In the end the job went to an outsider, as I knew it would – a friend of the managing director, someone told me. The day after Brenda and I had had our little chat about de Sade, Mrs Williams called me into her office to tell me I hadn't got the job. She had wanted to employ me, she said, but Management didn't think I had quite enough experience for such a senior position. That was complete bull, of course. The real reason was that they knew I wouldn't be just another "Yes" man. I made that very clear in the interview when I told Mrs Williams exactly what was wrong with the finance department and what needed to be done to put it right. It needed a firm hand on the tiller, I said, a firm hand like mine, but I knew even at the time that she wasn't convinced.

It wasn't long after I got turned down for the job as senior clerk that I started thinking seriously about how I could make a name for myself and move up in the world. It was obvious that I wouldn't be going far with Thompsons, no matter how hard I tried because my face didn't fit. That meant I either had to find another job or do something else. That was when I first gave myself to the dream that came true of stealing the company payroll. The idea had come to me out of the blue, about a week after Mrs Williams had called me into her office.

What happened was this. It was Friday lunchtime and I happened to be out in the yard when the weekly security van arrived with the wages. The driver and his partner parked outside the management building; took the money-box up to the wages office then stayed on for a cup of tea, which is what they did most weeks. It was all very relaxed because Thompsons was the last stop on their route, so there wasn't any more money to deliver. I don't think the driver thought it was all that important, leaving the van unattended, I mean, because there wasn't any cash inside, but it suddenly struck me that their security was incredibly lax. I remember thinking that they deserved to get ripped off just to teach them a lesson, which is how I got around to the idea of doing the job myself.

I think you should know that when I first began thinking about how to steal the company payroll, I'd already given a lot of thought to the idea of robbing a bank, which in my opinion, is a much more glamorous and exciting thing to do. I mean, imagine walking into a branch of Barclays and shouting, "Hands up! This is a robbery!" and then strolling out with a bag full of cash. The trouble is, when you look at exactly what's involved in a bank robbery you realise that it's not that simple. To start with, how do you know if the bank's actually got any money to steal? Then there are security cameras, bullet-proof glass and time locks to contend with, not to mention the fact that one of the customers might try to become a hero and cause all sorts of additional problems.

What I'm trying to say is that the idea of stealing some money didn't just happen, it was more the culmination of a series of events, something I'd been considering in the abstract for quite a few years and meeting Brenda was the last piece of the puzzle, the catalyst, so to speak, though I didn't realise it at the time. I also want to say that all the killing that happened later on wasn't planned either; it just came out of the blue.

The next time I had a real conversation with Brenda was about two weeks after we'd talked in my office. It was a Saturday morning and I'd gone for a walk after breakfast. I used to go walking quite often at weekends. Some weekends I'd go window-shopping in the High Street and at other times I'd take a drive out into the country and go hiking in the hills, but that particular morning I hadn't wanted to get in my car so I'd strolled through Ravenshill housing estate and across the Tenscore, which is a big piece of flat land laid out with soccer pitches, and had ended up in West Park down by the river.

It was a March day, I remember, but very cold so there weren't that many people about. Most of the trees were still bare from the winter. Only one or two were beginning to bud, small green shoots bright against the bark.

Brenda was wrapped up against the chill. She was wearing a long, black leather coat and a big red woollen ski hat pulled down low over her ears, which is why I didn't recognise her until we almost literally bumped into each other. She had a small brown dog in her arms and looked very upset.

If I had spotted her earlier, I would have turned around and gone the other way. Knowing what I know now though, I have to say that I think it's amazing how important a chance encounter like that can sometimes be to a person's life. Brenda always says that it was fate, the two of us meeting like that, but I don't believe in that kind of thing. What I do know is that if it hadn't been for that one chance meeting we'd probably never have got together and then both our futures would have been completely different.

When I first saw Brenda I felt awkward, which is why I mumbled something about not realising that she lived in that area. I don't know why I felt embarrassed but I did. That was why I couldn't think of anything better to say.

She shook her head, which I took to mean she didn't – live around there, I mean. That's when I noticed her eyes were all red and blotchy. When she finally managed to speak, she sounded like she had a lump in her throat.

"I came to visit my aunty and to take Merlin for a walk," she said.

That was when I took a closer look at the dog she was carrying. It seemed all limp and sleepy and there were flecks of pink foam around its mouth, but apart from that it didn't look hurt or injured in any way.

When I asked her if there was something wrong with the dog, she started shaking. That's when I felt myself go red all over again, though

I'm not sure Brenda noticed. All she kept doing was looking down at the dog and stroking the top of its head.

"I was taking him for a walk. He ran into the road and a car hit him. Now he's hardly moving."

Her eyes were suddenly all watery. Then a tear ran down her cheek.

"I don't know what to do," she said.

"I think you should take it to a vet," I said.

From the look on her face, you'd have thought I'd just made the most brilliant suggestion in the world. But then just as quickly, all the light went out of her and she looked pitiful again.

"I don't know where to find one," she said.

I knew there was an animal hospital not far away. I could have pleaded ignorance, of course, but I knew that if I didn't do something, I'd probably never hear the end of it.

"There's a place two streets away," I said, waving my hand in the general direction we'd have to go. That was when I asked if she wanted me to take her there. I regretted asking even before all the words were out of my mouth and I was hoping she'd turn me down, but she looked up at me, a little smile all around her eyes, looking relieved and thankful at the same time.

"Please," she said.

We set off together, hardly talking. Most of the time she was preoccupied with the dog and kept speaking to it, saying everything was going to be alright and things like that.

When we got to the vet's surgery we sat side by side in the waiting room, across the room from a man and a woman. The woman had a big black cat inside a metal cage. All the time we were sitting there, the cat kept twisting and turning, like it was demented, never once stopping, not even for a second. The man, who was reading the paper, had a Labrador sitting at his feet. Every time the nurse or the receptionist went in or out of the surgery, the dog would lift its head up to see what was going on, but the man didn't pay the slightest attention until his name was called.

I'd never been that close to Brenda before, all I can remember is the lovely smell of her perfume. Hypnotic Poison, I later found out it was called.

We had to wait half an hour for our turn, then the receptionist called Brenda's name and she went in to see the vet while I stayed out in the waiting room. Twenty minutes later she came out again. I could see that she had been crying again.

"The vet says that Merlin has internal injuries and is very badly hurt," she said. "I have to come back for him in the morning." Then she burst into tears. I was embarrassed because I hated public shows of emotion, but after an awkward moment, I put my arm around her and she leant her head against my shoulder. Her hair felt very soft and I remember that it smelt of fresh flowers.

"Do you want me to take you for a cup of tea?" I asked, because I couldn't think of anything else to say.

She nodded, which I took for a yes, so we went to a small café that I knew. I bought two cups of tea and an iced bun, which we shared.

"You always keep yourself to yourself, don't you, Matthew?" she said when she'd managed to stop sniffling.

I have to say that Brenda sometimes had the ability to put me on the defensive. She just had a special way about her that made me say things I wouldn't normally say and do things I wouldn't normally do. I think it was because she was so straightforward about private and personal matters. There were no sacred cows, so to speak, where Brenda was concerned.

"Is that such a crime?" I asked.

I was determined not to let things get too pally, which is why I spoke quite sharply, though I don't think she noticed.

"No," she said, shrugging her shoulders, "but it means you never get to know anyone, not properly anyway."

It was on the tip of my tongue to say, "I'm a loner. I don't want to get to know anyone properly or otherwise," but I knew it would sound stupid, so in the end I just took a sip of tea and didn't say anything.

Even when I was at school I never had any friends because I kept myself to myself. I always felt I was on the outside of everything, looking in. Still, every cloud has a silver lining, doesn't it? In my experience people can be very disappointing, so not having a lot of friends can turn out to be an advantage in the end, can't it? I mean, if you're more detached from people you tend to become more self-reliant and you get toughened up, which means you can take life's little knocks a lot better. You also become more objective because you don't have a lot of different people influencing you with their opinions.

I once heard two of my teachers talking about me and one of them whispered that she thought I was a loner. I think she thought I'd be upset if I heard her say the word out loud, but the truth is I was pleased. I think loners are special. You only have to think about Shane, the character from Jack Shaefer's book, to know that.

Shane was a gunfighter, a tough guy, but no one knew that because he seemed so ordinary. One afternoon he just appeared in a valley where some homesteaders were having trouble with the local cattle baron. At first he didn't get involved, then, when all the trouble started, he sided with the farmers. Shane was mysterious and dangerous, but he knew right from wrong and had a kind of inner strength that you didn't know was there until you got on the wrong side of him.

Shane was my hero when I was at school and there was a time when I was going to change my name to Shane when I grew up. I wanted to be more like him, you see. I never did, of course – change my name to Shane, I mean – but sometimes, when things happened to me, I'd say to myself, "What would Shane do in this situation?" or "What would Shane say?" and then I'd try to do the same. Like when the other kids at school called me names, I never retaliated, even though I wanted to. Sometimes I felt bad not doing anything, but being strong in the face of adversity is a special strength, if you want my opinion. Sometimes I think about going back to my old school and telling everyone what I've done, to show them what I've achieved, but I can't do that. Not now. Not for a lot of reasons.

"Don't you want to get to know the people you work with?" she asked.

I don't like answering questions. Normal people like Brenda always seem to think that it's alright to ask almost complete strangers about anything they please, even intimate personal things.

I poured myself another cup of tea and fussed over the milk and sugar because I didn't want her to see how angry I was.

"I prefer my own company," I said, not looking at her.

I thought she'd get the message from the way I answered, but she just looked more interested.

"Why's that?" she asked.

I gave her a sharp look so she could see I wanted to drop the subject, but it didn't make any difference. She just sat staring at me across the table, waiting for me to answer, like she'd just asked a perfectly normal question. But Brenda's very innocent about the ways of the world. You can tell that because even though she's quite pretty, she doesn't spend all her time at work primping herself like a beauty queen, which is what all the other pretty girls at Thompsons seem to do.

I could tell that she wasn't going to let the subject drop until she'd got an answer of some sort. In the end I said that most people either don't understand me, which means they usually misinterpret the things that I say, or they make fun of me.

She looked surprised. "But then you have to explain things to them!" she said.

At first I thought she was making fun of me, then I realised she was serious.

"That's easier said than done," I said. "I don't have the same interests as anyone at work. That means I'm not like all the others. In this world if you're seen as different, you're a freak. Mostly, people make fun of freaks."

"I don't think you're a freak," she said quite seriously. "I think you're very nice. You've been very kind to Merlin and me today."

I took a sip of tea and didn't reply. I'd never had that kind of conversation before. I knew that most people dismissed me as boring, or unfeeling, or something similar. That was the reason I didn't tell Brenda that I didn't give a damn about Merlin, or any other animals for that matter. I know that a dog's supposed to be man's best friend and all that, but I don't care for them.

After we'd finished our teas, we went outside and said goodbye on the pavement. She was going back to her aunt's place to tell her the bad news and I was going home.

"I'll see you at work on Monday," she said.

"I hope your dog's better by then," I said because I thought that was the kind of thing an ordinary person would say.

"Thank you," she answered, then turned to walk up the street. Before she went around the corner at the end of the road, she looked back at me and waved.

FOUR

AT WORK THE FOLLOWING Monday I stayed in my office all morning and kept my head buried in some papers. Out of the corner of my eye, I saw Brenda come to work, but I didn't go out to speak to her because I didn't want her to think that we were friends all of a sudden, just because we'd had a cup of tea together. She was wearing a red dress that I'd never seen before and her hair was tied back in a ponytail. She had on red lipstick too, and I got the impression that she'd made a special effort to look nice. When I saw her looking my way a couple of times during the morning, I pretended to be absorbed in something and ignored her.

When the other girls went over to the canteen at lunchtime, she came into my office and sat down without being asked.

"Have I done something wrong, Matthew?"

I acted surprised. "Done something wrong? I don't know what you mean."

Then she said, like she was accusing me, "You've ignored me this morning."

Suddenly I was on the defensive, which wasn't the way the exchange was supposed to go. I'd planned it all out in my head, you see. I'd be very businesslike and tell her that I was sorry about her dog, but that we would have to keep all personal matters away from work. That was an easy let-down for her and a good out for me and no one's feelings would get hurt. But instead of that I started to go red. I couldn't help it.

I explained that I'd been very busy and hadn't noticed her come to work, but it sounded feeble. She gave me a long stare. I didn't think she was going to let the matter rest, but she suddenly changed the subject.

"Aunty was very upset – about Merlin, I mean."

That was when I asked her how her dog was.

She let her face sink forward and her shoulders started to move. It was only when I heard her sniff that I realised she was crying. After

29

about a minute she took a handkerchief out of her sleeve and wiped her nose. Then she pulled herself together.

"The vet couldn't help him. He said Merlin was too badly hurt inside. In the end he put him to sleep."

I said that I was sorry and she nodded her head, grateful for my concern.

Out in the office, one of the other girls was standing next to her desk, watching us, but the moment she saw me looking at her, she took whatever it was that she had come back from the canteen to collect and went out again. I knew that a story about the two of us would be round the factory in ten minutes. I didn't like so much scrutiny and it made me furious to think there would soon be all sorts of rumours flying about the place.

"What's wrong?" Brenda asked, seeing the look on my face. She hadn't noticed the other girl come and go.

I didn't want to get into a conversation about it, especially since the damage had already been done, so I said that there wasn't anything wrong. I knew that wasn't going to be the end of it, though.

"Then why are you so cool towards me today?" she asked.

I wondered why she couldn't take a hint.

"I don't know what you're talking about," I said, irritated.

I thought she was going to start crying again, but she just blew her nose.

"On Saturday you were friendly," she said. "Now you're angry and won't even talk to me."

"I'm not angry," I said. Then I had a brainwave, "I'm just upset about your dog."

She hadn't expected that, I could tell by her expression. She gave me a curious look and then began to dry her eyes.

"But why do you care?" she said.

"Because I love animals," I said.

I thought it was the kind of thing she'd want to hear.

I couldn't help thinking the whole thing was ridiculous, though. This was exactly the reason why I'd acted the way I had, in order to avoid this kind of inane conversation, I mean. The girls in the typing pool were always talking about "love" and "relationships" and "making a commitment" and things like that and sometimes when I listened to them, it felt like I'd suddenly been transported into an episode from *The Bold and the Beautiful* or one of the other stupid soap operas.

"Do you have a dog then?" she asked.

I said that I'd grown up with dogs, which is why I was so fond of them.

Sometimes I'm amazed at how easily I can lie when I have to.

"Merlin was a lovely dog," she said.

"Yes, he was a lovely dog," I agreed.

When I thought she was composed again I explained very quietly that I didn't think it was good policy to mix one's work life and one's social life, which is why I hadn't said much that morning.

I could see that she was still upset, but I knew that couldn't be helped. It was better, I said, to be open and straightforward about things right from the start. That way there wouldn't be any unpleasantness or misunderstanding later on.

"I have to get back to my work now," I said and started shuffling some papers on my desk like I had a lot to do. I heard her chair scrape when she stood up, but I didn't look up again until I knew she was gone. I didn't want her to keep coming into my office, mooning over me all the time, or getting the idea that I was interested in her. I suppose you could say I was being cruel to be kind.

I thought that would be the end of it, but I was wrong. If anything, Brenda became more interested than ever. For a couple of days she kept away from my office, though I caught her looking at me from time to time. I suppose most men would have been flattered to be getting so much attention, but I didn't like it. I didn't want to create a situation at work that was likely to turn out embarrassing in the end. And I didn't want to be the talking point of the factory with everyone pointing fingers at me and sniggering behind my back. It wasn't that I disliked Brenda, in fact just the opposite was true, it was just that I had big plans for the future and she wasn't part of them.

After I'd explained my position about relationships at work, I felt a lot more comfortable, because we'd cleared the air so to speak. That's why I eventually made an effort to be a bit more friendly, saying "Good morning" and "How are you, Brenda?" and that sort of thing when we happened to bump into each other. Of course some of the other girls put two and two together and got five, getting it into their heads that we were "an item", as they called it. When I explained very clearly that this wasn't the case, one of them accused me of "toying with Brenda's affections", which was completely ridiculous, of course.

Although I'd made my position abundantly clear, after a while Brenda took to buying me small presents. Nothing too conspicuous mind you, a packet of chewing gum one day, a bar of chocolate another and so on. I always accepted the gifts gracefully, though without much enthusiasm, I have to say. What I mean is, I never encouraged her to buy me things, not once, although I was always polite.

Then she started popping into my office from time to time, usually at lunchtime. Even though the visits were always work-related, I made a point of being very cool towards her at first, until I was certain we'd developed the proper working relationship.

I have to admit though, that I didn't really discourage her in any way. This was because I didn't want to cause any friction or ill feeling, especially since I'd already made it quite clear how important I thought it was to separate home and work.

After a few weeks I let my guard down so to speak, not completely, of course, but I was a lot more tolerant. It was all very low key and innocent and even the other girls in the typing pool didn't seem that interested.

To tell you the truth, I felt quite sorry for Brenda. I don't think she had many friends, which is why I let things develop the way they did. I could understand how she felt, you see, being in the same position myself. Now I know that I shouldn't have got involved in the first place. Of course I didn't expect things to turn out the way they did, but it's always easy to be wise after the event, isn't it?

It wasn't until we really got talking that I realised just how ignorant she was. When I say ignorant, I don't mean ignorant in the sense that she couldn't read or write, because I'd learnt that she read quite a lot, I mean uninformed. For example, when I first mentioned Nietzsche she had no idea who I was talking about. That's why I started to lend her books. To educate her, I mean. I'd lend her a book one week and we'd talk about it the next.

I don't want you thinking that we were together all the time or always chatting about things, because that wasn't the case. In fact, we didn't spend that much time in each other's company. Over a couple of months I may have lent her three books and maybe once every two or three weeks we'd have a cup of tea together in my office. But it wasn't as if I was trying to run a proper educational course or anything like that.

I never thought of Brenda as a girlfriend, not at first anyway. She was a young woman and quite good looking, but I wasn't interested in starting up some kind of relationship or anything like that. For one thing, in my experience, most girls are very shallow creatures and they only see the surface of a person and not what's underneath, so they're not worth talking to. The girls in the typing pool were a typical example. They were always encouraging the men from the factory floor to come up and visit them. These were the kind of men who were loud-mouthed and crude – all mouth and trousers, as my Aunt Sal used to say – and they were always telling dirty jokes. I'm not narrow-minded, but I have better things to do than waste my time listening to stupid stories full of foul language, which is why I always stayed out of the way whenever I could. Jenny Martin once told me that I ought to stop being so stuck up and superior, but when I tried to explain to her that just because I liked to improve myself and didn't mix with the others, didn't mean that I was stuck up, she wouldn't listen and went off in a huff.

I'm pleased to say that the other girls didn't take much notice of us, not after a few weeks that is. They knew that Brenda and I occasionally had a cup of tea together, but it was nothing more than that and it wasn't often enough to create any real gossip. The fact is, there was nothing to gossip about. I didn't know anything about Brenda's background and she didn't know anything about mine, which is just the way I wanted to keep it. That's because we never talked about friends and family and that sort of thing. When we met we'd only talk about things of mutual interest, or the books I'd lent her.

I must admit that I was pleasantly surprised to discover that Brenda had a much better mind than I thought, incisive, really. What I mean is she'd sometimes say things I didn't expect. Like the time I was telling her about Nietzsche's "Superman" and she asked me how a person would know if he or she was superior. I was surprised at the time because I didn't think she was really following what I was saying.

"That person would just know," I said.

At first she just stared at me, then she looked away and I saw her eyes narrow slightly, almost like she was making up her mind about something.

"Is that how you see yourself," she asked. "As a Superman, I mean?"

I didn't answer straight away. Not because I didn't know what to say, but because I didn't know what her reaction would be.

By the way, that's another thing I find interesting about Brenda: even though she's a woman I'm never quite sure what she's thinking.

"Yes," I said. I didn't add that I'd always known I was special, even from the time I was little.

I half expected her to argue the point, or make some kind of cynical reply, but she just nodded, like what I'd said was the most logical thing in the world. Then she picked up a pencil from my desk and began tapping it against her knee.

"I thought so," she said after a long pause.

I waited for her to say something else, but she just seemed to drift off into thought again. I felt I needed to explain so I said that saying such a thing might sound arrogant, but that wasn't what I meant.

She started nodding. "Yes, I know," she replied, then fell silent again.

After that we changed the subject and talked about work. Then ten minutes later she said something I hadn't been expecting.

"If you're one of Nietzsche's Supermen, you don't think you have to stick to the same rules and regulations as everyone else, do you?"

That was when I realised that all the time we'd been talking about work, she'd been thinking about something else.

"No, you don't," I answered. "Ordinary rules don't apply to some people."

"Then why are you working here? Why are you doing this job? Why aren't you doing something more... more worthy of yourself?"

For a moment I thought she was making fun of me, then I saw that it was a genuine inquiry.

"It's to do with circumstances," I explained. "I have to wait for the right opportunity to come along."

"You have to make opportunity happen," she said.

That was when I told her I had big plans for the future. Even before the words were all out my mouth though, I knew it sounded like I was making excuses.

"We all have big plans. The important thing is what you do with them."

"I'm already putting my plans into action," I said.

When she asked me to tell her what I was talking about, I wouldn't answer. It was a secret, I said. She looked very sceptical at first and made a comment about me trying to avoid the issue, but I just shrugged and stayed mum. That was when she started to become insistent. She wouldn't let the matter drop, but I refused to say anything else because I wanted her to realise that there were things going on in my life that she didn't know about. It was too soon, I thought, to tell her I was planning to bite the hand that fed me, so to speak. I didn't know her well enough for one thing, and there were still some details to work out. In the end, she got quite angry and I don't think she would have let up until she'd gotten the full story out of me except the hooter went off in the factory to signal the end of lunchtime and she had to go back to her desk.

I remember that conversation very clearly because she was so determined and insistent. It was a side of Brenda I'd never seen before.

FIVE

IT WAS A WEEK LATER that I asked Brenda if she wanted to go out for the evening. There was a film festival on at the local cinema, a collection of Nazi propaganda films that had been made in Germany during the 1930s. On the last day of the festival, there was a panel discussion with a group of experts, which I wanted to go to.

I gave the matter a lot of thought before I invited her along. I mean it wasn't as if we were bosom buddies or anything, we'd just had one or two interesting conversations. What I'm saying is that I didn't have any intention of getting romantically involved – that just happened. I simply enjoyed having someone to talk to and it made a change to be taken seriously for once. Anyway, when I finally asked her agreed yes straight away.

She had heard about Hitler and the Nazis, of course, but I was surprised how little she knew about them. I told her about the Second World War and the Holocaust and that kind of thing. "The Nazis are an example of a group that has enforced its will over others," I said. Brenda said they were cruel and immoral and ruled by fear, but I told her that this didn't matter because they had worked their way into power by getting a large section of the German population to support them. "Morality doesn't come into it," I said, but Brenda didn't agree. Even when I explained to her that because the Nazis had been able to take control of Germany it proved that they were superior and this gave them the right to do as they wished, she argued the point. "Might doesn't mean right," she said.

That was the first time I realised how strong-willed she could be.

Anyway, we made an arrangement to meet outside the cinema at a quarter to three the following Sunday afternoon. I said that I thought it best if we didn't tell anyone at work that we were going out together because Management frowned on that sort of thing. (I didn't say exactly what I meant by "that sort of thing" and she didn't ask.)

I was surprised when she said, "Oh, yes, you're absolutely right," because I was expecting her to object to the idea. Then she added, "Anyway, the other girls would only be jealous and make stupid comments."

I knew she was talking about me but I didn't ask her what the other girls would be jealous about because I wasn't used to having young women pay me compliments.

We'd arranged to meet at the cinema at a quarter to three, but I made a point of turning up fifteen minutes late, just as the film was about to start. To be honest, I'd had second thoughts about the whole thing and nearly didn't turn up at all. In the end, the only reason I went along was because I knew that if I didn't my name would be muck around the factory. Later, Brenda told me that she'd got there early and had been waiting for nearly half an hour. Actually, I knew that anyway because I spied on her from a shop doorway up the road for fifteen minutes before I strolled over, but I pretended to be surprised. If she had walked away, I was going to run up to her all breathless and apologise for being late, like I'd just spotted her leaving, but that wasn't necessary. To be quite honest, I think she would have waited for another hour if she thought I would've turned up in the end.

When I said I was sorry for keeping her waiting, she just smiled and said it didn't matter. I thought it was the right thing to do to make her wait a little. That way I didn't seem too eager and it also made it very clear exactly who was the boss, if you know what I mean.

Anyway, Brenda took my arm as we walked up to the ticket office, like we were boyfriend and girlfriend. I know my face was as red as a beetroot because I was worried that someone from work would see us, but I realised there was nothing I could do about that so I just pretended that having a girl hanging on my arm was the most normal thing in the world, though it was an effort to keep calm. Brenda seemed quite relaxed about the whole thing, though. She even offered to buy her own ticket, but I told her that it was my treat.

Inside, the cinema was almost empty. Underneath the screen there was a lectern and a long table and some chairs for the panel of experts.

A professor somebody-or-other stood up before the lights went out and explained that the two films we were going to see had been commissioned by the Nazis to encourage anti-Jewish feeling. They were used to mould public opinion in Germany, he said. Then he went on for about ten minutes about the power of propaganda. He was too fond of the sound of his own voice, for my liking, but he eventually sat down and the show began.

Both films were in black and white and were very grainy, showing their age. The first one showed the Jews living in filth and surrounded by rats. Even I knew that everything was exaggerated and that things weren't like that, but I admired the Nazis for their meticulous effort in putting together a film that was so powerful.

Brenda put her arm through mine while we watched the films, but we didn't talk at all. After the first film was over, there was a short intermission and I got us both an ice cream, which we ate in silence.

The second film was about the German Hitler-Jugend, which was set up by Adolf Hitler in 1933 for educating and training German boys in Nazi principles. The professor said that when a boy reached his tenth birthday, he was registered and investigated for racial purity and then inducted into the German Young People organisation. When he was 13 he became eligible for the Hitler Youth, which he stayed in until he was 18, then he joined the Nazi party. Girls joined a different organisation called the League of German Girls, where they were trained for comradeship, domestic duties and motherhood.

What impressed me about the film was the way Hitler had set the whole thing up. Everyone looked so fit and healthy and happy yet they were all behaving like robots. It was interesting to me to see how easy it was to make people do what you wanted.

When the films were over there was a panel discussion and members of the audience were given a chance to join in and ask questions. Most of the people on the panel were long-haired types who came from the university, although there was one film-director who talked about some of the technical aspects of film-making.

I didn't take part in the talk, but Brenda asked a question about why the films had been so effective and this led to a long discussion about what propaganda is and how it works.

When we got outside at seven o'clock, I was ready to go home, but

Brenda wanted to go for a cup of coffee and I didn't feel that I could say no, not having invited her in the first place and then kept her waiting, that is. The truth was I hadn't enjoyed the films that much and I'd got angry when Brenda had asked her question. I couldn't help it. She made me feel small when I didn't say anything and she did. When she asked me why I hadn't joined in the discussion at the end, I just said I couldn't be bothered because I'd heard it all before. The truth is I find it hard to speak in front of people. Once, for example, I had to give a presentation at Thompsons and I ended up all tongue-tied and flustered, but then the managers I had to speak to were only out to humiliate me, so I suppose that was only to be expected.

I suggested a little café just around the corner, but Brenda offered to make me a cup of coffee at her flat, which was only about ten minutes' walk away. Her flatmate was away for the weekend, she said, so we would have the place to ourselves, which would make it easier for us to talk. I wasn't that keen, but she seemed insistent, so in the end I said okay.

She lived in a big, three-storey Victorian house that had been converted into three separate apartments, one to each floor. Her flat, which was on the top floor, consisted of a lounge, a small kitchen, a bathroom and two bedrooms. The lounge, which was at the front of the house, had a big bay window that looked down onto the street and an old cut-glass chandelier hanging on a long brass chain from the ceiling. From the entrance hall, there was a dark passageway that led past the kitchen and the bathroom to the two bedrooms at the back of the house.

The place was "homely"; at least I think that's the word that most people would use. In the lounge, for example, there was a white three-piece suite covered with big, fluffy cushions, a small bookcase, a glass-topped coffee table and a TV. Brenda and her flatmate had painted the walls maroon and there was a tall up-lighter lamp in one corner, so the room had a kind of dark, romantic look about it. It was just the sort of place where you'd expect to find two girls living. My flat is very Spartan by comparison, because I don't have any carpets. Nor do I have much furniture, only a table and a couple of hard chairs in the living room and a bed and bedside table in the bedroom. I don't have a television either, but I do have a radio that I listen to quite often. There are tall stacks of books on the floor in the lounge and the bedroom, but the place is never untidy because I make a point of keeping it spotlessly clean.

Brenda told me to make myself comfortable and then vanished into the kitchen to make a hot drink. While she was away, I looked in the bookcase. It was just what I expected, full of trashy romantic novels, with titles like, "Lost Love" or "A Weekend of Memories" and that sort of thing. Later, Brenda told me that they all belonged to her flatmate.

After five minutes she brought out a tray containing two cups of coffee plus a matching milk jug and sugar bowl. I could tell straightaway that they were her "best" things and that she'd made a special effort on my behalf.

"You know I like you a lot, don't you," she said after she had put the tray down.

I didn't reply at first because I didn't know what to say. After all, it was a surprising thing to blurt out. We hadn't been out together before and the only time we'd talked was at work, but women are unpredictable creatures so perhaps I should have expected it.

To give myself more time to think I said that I didn't know what she meant.

She frowned at me, considering just how to answer.

"I mean, you're so well read. You understand the world."

At first I thought she was back-pedalling, trying to take back what she'd said, then I realised she was merely clarifying a point. She was staring at me, waiting to see my reaction.

" I like to know what's going on in the world," I answered.

"What I want to know is, do you like me?" she asked.

I suddenly felt all hot and flustered. I didn't like the direction the conversation was taking. I nearly said, haven't I made it clear from the start that I'm not looking for a romantic relationship, but I knew that was the wrong thing to say, so I kept quiet to give myself time to think. I suppose I could have reminded her that because we worked together it wasn't a good idea to form any kind of emotional attachment, but in the end, I decided to take the line of least resistance.

"Yes, I like you," I said, which was just the answer she was looking for.

"Good, then let's drink our coffee in bed."

Without waiting for me to answer, she picked up the tray and walked down the corridor to her bedroom. When she realised I wasn't following, she came back and stood in the doorway.

"Well, are you coming or not?" she said.

She didn't leave me much choice in the matter, not really, anyway, so I got up and followed her. It would have looked stupid if I'd done anything else. The trouble was, this wasn't how I'd planned for things to turn out. That's not to say I hadn't considered the idea of a physical relationship with a woman, it was just that I hadn't expected that sort of intimacy to happen so quickly, after I'd only known a person for such a short time, I mean.

The last time I had been with a woman was about a year before. One night when I was feeling lonely, I'd phoned a massage parlour that was advertising in the local paper. The girl on the other end said that a "personal massage" at home would cost me £50. After I'd agreed to the price she took my address and said she'd be at my place in about half an hour. Two hours later a man and woman knocked on my door. First the man looked me over then he said he'd go and wait in the car until we'd finished.

After I'd paid her the £50 she asked me what I wanted. I wasn't quite sure what she meant. "I mean do you want to screw me?" she said and I could see that she was angry for some reason.

I asked her if she was the woman I'd spoken to, though I knew that she wasn't. The woman on the telephone had sounded very nice. Kind and helpful, I mean and quite young, not bad-tempered, not someone with bleached hair and thick caked-on make-up, someone who was old enough to be my mother.

I could see that the question had made her even angrier.

"We're all the same lying down, love," she said and started taking off her clothes. When she saw me standing there, watching her, she shook her head.

"I haven't got all night, you know," she said, all irritable.

She lay on her back on the bed with her legs open and then gave me a condom. "You need to use this," she said, but by then all the desire had gone so trying to get it on was a futile exercise, if you know what I mean. I couldn't do anything after that, though I didn't try very hard to be truthful and after about ten minutes she got up, put her clothes back on and left without saying a word.

When I walked into the bedroom, Brenda was already taking off her dress. She had closed the curtains so the place was quite dark and had put the tray on a sideboard and I got the impression that coffee was the last thing on her mind at that moment.

By the time I'd untied my shoelaces she had already slipped into bed. With the blankets pulled up around her neck she said, "I hope you don't think I make a habit of this."

I felt too nervous to speak taking off my shirt like that, so I just shook my head but didn't answer. After I'd folded my clothes I put them on a chair, then got into bed. I left my underpants and socks on because the room was cold.

The moment I lay down Brenda was all over me. First she was kissing me on the lips, and then she put her tongue inside my mouth, which no one had ever done to me before. When I put my hand on her breast she closed her eyes and started moaning and groaning, then she took my other hand and put it between her legs. She seemed completely carried away, like she was in another world or something. I pretended that I knew exactly what I was doing and remembering what the massage parlour woman had said to me, told her that I didn't have any protection on me. I would have been relieved if she'd stopped suddenly and said, "Oh, then we can't go any further," but she just shrugged and said, "I've taken care of everything, Matt."

I nearly told her that my name was Matthew not Matt, but it didn't seem quite the right moment.

After she'd helped me take off my underpants, she put her hand on my private to make it stand up, but I suppose you could say I wasn't feeling amorous. When that didn't work, she pushed me onto my back and then knelt over me, and put her mouth over it. Up until then I thought that the only women who did that kind of thing were women of ill repute, if you know what I mean, not ordinary girls.

I got hard before too long, then Brenda lay back and pulled me on top of her and helped me do what I had to do. She started thrashing around again, but much louder this time. After about five minutes it was all over for the both of us. We didn't smoke a cigarette like they do in the films, we drank a cup of coffee instead. Then I got up and went home.

Six

ALL THE NEXT DAY the only thing I could think about was what had happened the night before. As I've said already, I didn't think it was a good idea to have a relationship with a work colleague, so it bothered me that if I started seeing Brenda it would mean going against my principles. In my opinion, a man who sacrifices his principles isn't worth anything. In the end though, I compromised because I could see she was different to other girls at work. That was one of the reasons I liked her, her uniqueness, I mean, although her behaviour, which was quite unpredictable at times, occasionally left something to be desired. It was also obvious that she had strong feelings for me and I didn't want her causing some kind of scene if I ignored her.

I don't want you getting the impression that I didn't like Brenda, because that isn't the case. By this time I was quite fond of her, it was just I was concerned that our personal relationship might have a detrimental effect at work.

After giving the matter careful consideration, I wrote her a note saying that I thought we should go on seeing each other, but that it would be better if we kept our relationship private, in order to avoid the wagging tongues. The next morning I put the note in a folder with some papers she had brought to my office a few days before and stuck it on her desk so that she'd find it when she got to work.

I wasn't sure what her reaction would be, though I knew there was a chance she might not like the idea of us keeping the whole thing quiet, I mean. As it turned out I couldn't have been more wrong. At tea break that morning, she came into my office on the pretext of bringing me a letter to sign and said that she thought that what I had suggested was a good idea.

"The girls here don't know when to shut up," she whispered, meaning they were always sticking their noses into other peoples' business, which I had to agree with, of course.

We made a point of keeping our distance after that and only met when there was a genuine work-related reason. I don't think anyone else at Thompsons had the slightest idea that we were going out together, which was to prove to our advantage in the end, but I'll get to that in due course.

Outside of work, we began to see a lot more of each other, which was inevitable I suppose, considering what we had done together. At first I started to go around to her flat two or three times a week. Most times we'd have sex if the flat was empty, which was quite often because her flatmate also had a boyfriend and she often used to stay with him overnight, especially at weekends. Sometimes she wouldn't be there for a week at a time, even.

I have to confess that Brenda was very uninhibited where sex was concerned and we ended up doing all sort of things, even videoing ourselves, which I was uncomfortable with at first, though I got into it more later on.

"You're very self-conscious, aren't you?" she said on one occasion.

"I'm just not so free and easy as you are about certain things," I said, defending myself.

"Fucking isn't dirty, it's just a very natural activity carried out by two people."

"Swearing like that makes me very angry. I'd prefer it if you didn't use that kind of language," I said, very sharply.

"Whatever you say," she said and then changed the subject to talk about something else.

It wasn't long after we'd started going out that Brenda brought up the subject of us living together. Expecting her to argue the point, I said that I didn't think it was such a good idea. She just shrugged her shoulders and said that she also thought that things were okay as they were.

"Then why did you bring up the subject in the first place?" I asked.

"Because I just needed to know that we both feel the same way," she said, which didn't make all that much sense to me, to be honest.

That's not to say that living separately didn't cause problems from time to time. On one occasion, for example, Gloria from work dropped in at Brenda's unexpectedly and I had to hide in the bedroom for an hour until she'd gone.

I don't want you thinking that Brenda just does everything I tell her, because that isn't the case. She has a mind of her own and she can be very insistent about some things, especially when she gets stuck on an idea, but I always have the final say. Always. I insist on that because she tends to get carried away by the enthusiasm of the moment, if you know what I mean, whereas I'm much more down-to-earth and level-headed.

After we'd been going out for a couple of weeks, I realised that I didn't know that much about her, which is why I asked her about previous boyfriends one night. We were at her place – as usual – sitting in the lounge watching a boring film on TV, but the moment I brought up the subject I saw her whole demeanour change. It was almost like she was drawing back into herself. I was surprised because she's usually so open and talkative.

"You don't want to talk about it, do you?" I asked.

I was pressing her because I knew I'd touched a nerve.

"No, I don't," she answered, not looking at me.

"We shouldn't keep secrets from one another."

She turned to stare at me. "Then you tell me about your girlfriends," she snapped, almost like it was a challenge.

I made like the whole thing was no big deal. "There's nothing to tell," I answered. "There's never been anyone special, not before you, anyway."

There was a long pause before she said anything. "I've only had one real boyfriend before you," she said. "His name was Paul. We only went out together for a few weeks."

"What happened?" I asked.

"He went to live in another town so we split up."

She'd tried to be casual about the whole thing, but I knew she was lying, or at least not telling me the whole truth.

My guess is that Brenda's had lots of boyfriends, but maybe the Paul she'd mentioned was special. He probably dumped her, which is why she didn't want to talk about him, so I didn't pursue the point.

She didn't say much about her family either. I knew she was an only child, like me, and that she'd grown up in London. Her mother and father had died very young, she said, and she'd been brought up in an orphanage, which was why she had moved up north, because she didn't want to remember a lot of unhappy memories, she said.

"Then who's your aunt," I said, "the one with Merlin?"

"She was a friend of my parents."

When I started asking questions about them, she became weepy so I dropped the subject. "The wound was still very raw," she said, which was why she'd never told me anything about them in the past.

I was born in the Midlands, but I grew up in Lancashire. I never knew my father because my mother ran off and left him about a month after I was born. She never said much about those times, but I think he used to knock her about, which was the main reason she moved up north – to get away from his fists, I mean. Not that she ever said as much, but I know that because two years ago I went back to my home town to see the house where I was born and when I was standing outside in the street, one of the neighbours recognised me. I was the spitting image of my father, she said, which was how she knew who I was. Over a cup of tea she told me all about him – about his drunken binges and his violence and I just sat and listened, eating a Rich Tea biscuit and wishing I was somewhere else. That was when I learnt he was dead. A year before, he'd got knocked down by one of the trams on the new Wolverhampton to Birmingham line. Apparently he was drunk. The story was in the news at the time, but my mum never said anything so I still don't know if she knows that he's dead. Good riddance to bad rubbish, I say.

Anyway, after we moved away from the Midlands my father never tried to contact us again, nor did he pay my mum any money, so it was a real struggle for her to make ends meet. She got a job as a sales assistant in a fruit shop the day after we arrived in Manchester and worked there for years. It wasn't a very good job as jobs go, but it kept the wolf from the door, as my mum would say, and we always had fruit in the house. Not the best fruit, of course, only the speckled or bruised stuff that the customers didn't want to buy. That's why I won't eat any fruit that has any kind of mark or blemish on it now, because it brings back memories that I don't want to think about. It's one of my idiosyncrasies, I suppose. I know that shopkeepers sometimes get irritated with me when they see me examining their produce for even the slightest imperfection, but that's the way I am and I'm too old to change now.

When I was four years old I went to live with my aunt Sal and her husband, uncle Norman. Aunt Sal wasn't a real aunty, just a friend of my mum's who didn't have any children of her own. My mum had met another man, you see, and about a month after he moved in with us he told her that he didn't want a young kid cramping his style, so I had to move out.

I didn't see so much of my mum after that, though for about six months she used to come to visit me about once a week to bring me clothes and fruit and small treats and that sort of thing. Gordon, the man who had moved in with her, never came with her, of course, which was fine by me since I didn't like him. At first I kept asking my mum when I could move back home and she'd always say, "Soon, Matthew. As soon as I talk your uncle Gordon around," but that never happened, so after a time I just gave up asking.

After about a year my mum stopped coming to see me. I think my Aunt Sal had something to do with that because I once heard the two of them on the telephone and I could tell they were talking about me. Aunt Sal was saying that she didn't think it was a good idea for my mum to come and visit because I was always so upset when she left, which was true, but that didn't mean that I didn't want to see her. I know my mum argued the point, but my Aunt Sal was adamant so she might just as well have saved her breath, because when my Aunt Sal made up her mind about something there was no changing it. She was what some people call a "strong-willed" person, though "domineering" is a better word for her.

It was Aunt Sal who wore the trousers in the house, if you know what I mean. She was only five foot tall and Norman, her husband, was six foot six. He was a bricklayer by trade, a gentle giant with a big black bushy beard who was built like a brick shithouse, as Aunt Sal used to say. I hated it when she used that kind of vulgar language, but Aunt Sal was never one to worry much about what other people thought of her, me included. When she was angry or upset, which seemed to be most of the time, she had a way of looking at you with her head tilted slightly to one side and her eyes narrowed, that made you want to crawl under a stone.

Her hair was stone grey and she kept it pulled back off her face and fixed in a bun at the back of her neck. All day long you'd see her going to the mirror in the lounge to check that it was in place. Sometimes she'd loosen her hair, then lean backwards, arching her back and shaking her head from side to side like a big cat shaking water off its coat until it hung down to her waist in a long, grey sheet. Then she'd tie it up again, patting it down so that not even a hair was out of place. Sometimes she'd pull it so tight it would stretch back the skin around her eyes so there wasn't even a laughter line. Not that she ever laughed very much, mind you.

I never had much sympathy for uncle Norman who just seemed to pad around the house like a trained bear. Aunt Sal was always telling him what to do and all I ever heard him say was "Yes, Sal," or "I'll do that now, Sal". She often used to call him a big lummox and for a long time I thought a lummox was a huge, hairy animal, which in my opinion was a perfect description for him, but apparently a lummox is a stupid, clumsy person, which is also a description that suited him down to the ground.

Anyway, the moment I heard Aunt Sal telling my mum to stay away from me, I knew I wouldn't be seeing much more of her, which was exactly what happened. My mum stopped visiting and eventually I stopped asking about her. She and Gordon live in Northern Ireland now and I haven't seen them for years, though she does phone at Christmas and on my birthday, that sort of thing.

Actually, I try not to think too much about those early years. I knew that my mum had gone off and left me, of course, but I never cried about it. Not that I'd have gotten any sympathy from Aunt Sal even if I did. Aunt Sal, you see, could never tolerate anyone "snivelling," as she called it, because "snivelling" was a sign of weakness, and in her world, there were only two kinds of people – the strong and the weak – with nothing in between.

I suppose that was the time I first started to hide my feelings, when my mum stopped coming to visit me, I mean. I knew that some people felt sorry for me, of course, but I made a point of not feeling sorry for myself or letting anyone pity me, which was one of the reasons why I kept myself to myself at school, because I knew I was different to all the other kids, which is probably why I understand Brenda so well.

The one happy memory I have of school is the time one of the teachers organised a day trip to Snowdonia National Park in north

Wales. I was six or seven at the time. Most of the children had never been out of the city before – me included – nor had we ever seen a mountain, though Snowdon was a bit disappointing in that regard, if you want my opinion.

Anyway, early one Friday morning in spring we all got onto a coach and drove for about three hours. Eventually, we all piled out onto a car park, which was in a valley surrounded by a few trees. There was a lot of shouting and some of the boys started chasing after the girls, pinching them and making them squeal. After a time, the teachers organised us into class lines and Mr Links, the headmaster, pointed to the tallest green hill in the distance.

"That's Snowdon," he said.

He then went on to explain that Snowdon is a very old mountain and that it'd been worn away by what he called 'geological time', which is why it's not so high and there isn't always snow on the top.

Everyone had been told to bring good walking shoes and something to eat and drink. The plan was for us all to walk to the bottom of the mountain, where we'd have a picnic, but I suddenly wanted to go off on my own.

I'd never really been in the country before, and didn't want to share it with anyone, which sounds strange I know, but that's how I felt. I just wanted to be alone, to have some space to myself, so when everyone was about to leave, I went and hid in the bus. Afterwards, I had to climb out of a side window because the bus driver had locked up and gone off with the others.

It was very quiet, quieter than I'd ever known and the only thing I could hear were the birds. At first I just sat on a grass bank next to the coach, then I went for a walk down the valley. I ended up sitting on top of a low stone wall that separated one sheep field from the next. The sky was perfect that day, I remember, cloudless, like a big blue vault.

Eventually, I went back to the car park and waited for the others to arrive.

Of course, the teachers had a lot to say about me going off on my own and some of the other kids made fun of me, but I didn't care. I didn't argue or anything, because that's not my way. All the way home in the coach I just looked out of the window, thinking about how much I liked being alone. It was a kind of revelation, I suppose, knowing that I didn't need anyone else, I mean. When I look back on things, I often think that was the happiest day of my life.

After that school trip the teachers sometimes called me moody and sullen – those were the words they used – but I just wanted to be left alone. In fact, until I was a lot older, I always wondered why they couldn't accept that I wasn't like them, but that was stupid of me, wasn't it? After all, someone who's different always threatens people, don't they?

SEVEN

IT WAS ABOUT TWO WEEKS after we went to the cinema that I told Brenda about the plan I had to rob the company. We were in my office at the time. I was bending down at the filing cabinet, looking for a personnel file she wanted, pretending I couldn't find it. She was standing by my desk with her back to me, staring out into the Typing Pool.

"I've had enough of this place," I said quietly.

She shrugged, like it was something unimportant. "You won't get out of here unless you apply for other jobs," she said. By then she knew that I'd been turned down for the job of senior clerk.

"That's not what I mean," I said, trying to keep my voice low so no one else would hear.

She was fiddling with a stapler, shooting staples at the bin, not really listening.

"I don't know what you're talking about," she said.

"I'm talking about getting on in life," I said. "Things will never get better if we wait for others to give us what we want. That's a pipe dream. We must make our own opportunities."

That was a bit like stating the obvious, I suppose, so I wasn't surprised that she looked confused when she turned around.

"What do you mean?"

I explained that I was talking about doing something for myself.

"Doing something for yourself?" she asked. "You mean starting your own business, that kind of thing?"

I could see from her expression that she hadn't the foggiest idea what I was getting at.

I said, "Yes and no. Not a business, at least, not an ordinary business."

That was when she started to get irritated, but she could be like that sometimes, short-tempered, I mean.

Suddenly she was snappy. "You're not making any sense," she said.

I explained that I had given the matter a lot of thought. I was being held back by inferior people who were scared I'd show them up, which was why I hadn't got the job of senior clerk. It was the only explanation that made sense. That was why it was time I took matters into my own hands.

This time she pulled a face and banged the stapler down on the desk. "I still don't know what you mean," she said.

"I mean, it's time I made myself some decent money," I answered.

"Decent money," she repeated, cynical now.

"Yes."

She started to smile. I could tell she thought I was joking.

"What are we talking about here," she asked with a big grin on her face, "A bank robbery? A cash heist?"

She wasn't serious. She was just making fun of me.

"A cash heist," I said.

She rolled her eyes at the ceiling. "You're mad," she said.

That was when I told her I had a plan to rob the company payroll.

"Ordinary people don't rob banks," she said, like she was speaking to a child. That was when I started to get angry.

I said that we weren't ordinary people and that I wasn't talking about robbing a bank. I was talking about hijacking the security van that brought the wages on a Friday.

I think she would have laughed out loud, but she could see from the look on my face that I was deadly earnest.

"You've got to be kidding!" She was still grinning, but now she looked nervous too.

That's when I told her about my plan, about how I'd been watching the wages being delivered, how lax the security was and how, if I had a set of ignition keys, I'd have been able to stroll over and drive the van away long before anyone noticed.

When I said this to Brenda she said, "Yes, but you don't have a set, do you?"

"I know how to solve that problem, too," I said, "but I need a partner." Then I held out the personnel file that she'd come into my office to collect. She was staring at me, but there was a look on her face I couldn't fathom, a look I'd never seen before.

She took the file. "We'll talk about it tonight," she said and went back to her desk.

"How much money are we talking about?" Brenda asked, the minute I walked into her flat that night. I knew straight away that she'd been thinking about what I'd said. She was completely different to the way she'd been at work that morning. I mean, she was serious this time; she wasn't trying to make fun of me.

"All I know for certain is that the wages bill for Thompsons is usually about a hundred and fifty thousand pounds, and that there are other firms involved too," I said.

"What other firms?" she asked.

"The other firms that have their wages delivered on the same morning."

"How many are we talking about?"

"Three or four."

"So there's likely to be a lot more than a hundred and fifty thousand?"

"Yes."

"That's not bad."

I could tell she was imagining a big pile of cash.

" The money isn't important to me," I said.

"Then you're mad," she laughed.

"There are things more important than money," I said, but that just made her giggle all the more.

Eventually, she calmed down. "If we rob our own firm aren't we going to be the first people the police suspect?"

I'd thought about that. On a normal Friday, the security firm normally delivered wages to three other companies besides Thompsons. Even if the police thought one of these firms was involved they'd have at least four lots of staff to investigate, and that wasn't counting any ordinary criminals that might have done the job. As I said to her, I couldn't think of a reason why they'd suspect the two of us any more than they'd suspect anyone else.

"They will if they catch one of us driving the van away!" she said.

"Then we'll have to be very careful to make sure that they don't," I whispered.

She smiled at this bit of theatre, and I could see she wanted to believe in me, but she still wasn't entirely convinced.

"How are you going to get hold of the security van keys?" she asked after a long pause.

That was the tricky part, but I had a plan. "First we make the security van break down, then we go to the garage where it's being repaired and steal the ignition keys and make duplicates. After we've made copies we take the keys back to the garage and no one will be any the wiser."

She needed to think about this. We were in the kitchen at the time, making a cup of tea. The kettle started to boil and she turned away and began putting cups and saucers on a tray. Then she poured hot water into the teapot.

"So we make the truck break down, then we steal the ignition keys and make copies. Just like that." She was trying to be offhand, like she didn't really care, but I could tell from the way she was acting that she was excited about the idea.

"Yes," I said.

"But how do you know they'll take it to a garage? They might take it back to the depot where we can't get at it?"

She hadn't asked how we'd make it break down in the first place. That was a tricky part, too, but I didn't say anything. One thing at a time, was my motto.

I explained that a week before I'd overheard one of the drivers telling Mr Marsden, the head of finance, that he'd had to take the security van to the garage that morning, after he'd noticed an oil leak. He even mentioned the name of the garage he'd gone to.

"You've got this all worked out, haven't you?" she said, impressed.

"Not everything," I said, "but most things, yes."

"I need to think about it," she said.

After that she was quiet for most of the evening. When we were in bed later on she couldn't seem to get enough sex. Brenda was always enthusiastic about sex, but I hadn't seen her like that before. I think it was the idea of robbing the payroll that got her all excited for some reason. After we'd finished and were lying there exhausted, she turned to me.

"I've been thinking about what you said, Matthew," she whispered. "I think it's a good idea."

We went over the scheme a lot in the days that followed. Then we started making definite plans. At first it was more like a game than anything else, like we were playing cops and robbers, that sort of thing, but we both knew there was a serious side to what we were doing. It was exciting, but dangerous too, which was why I insisted we didn't leave anything to chance. I had no intention of ending up in prison because of a silly mistake or because we'd overlooked something basic.

One of the things we didn't know was the route the wages van took on its Friday run, so the following week I took time off work to find out. I was parked up the road from the security firm's depot before eight o'clock that morning and when the wages van left the depot at a quarter to nine, I was right behind.

After collecting money at the local bank, there were three deliveries, all to local factories and then they headed for Thompsons. The interesting thing was that the vehicle was left unattended at three out of the four stops, once for nearly fifteen minutes.

That confirmed what I'd thought about the company having lax security.

"All we have to do is wait for the right opportunity, then drive away with the money," I said to Brenda.

"If we've got the keys," she answered.

"Yes," I said – "if we've got the keys."

I could see her thinking about it, going over things in her mind. Then she said, "Where would we do it?"

"At Broads," I said, naming the factory where the wages van had stopped for the longest time.

She went silent again, for a lot longer this time. Eventually, she said, "Right," very business-like all of a sudden. That's when I knew she'd finally made up her mind.

"The next thing we have to do is to get hold of a set of van keys," I said,

I'd already worked out how to do that. The plan was simplicity itself, at least I thought so.

First we had to break into the yard where the security van was kept overnight and pour oil into the petrol tank. Then, the next day, we had to follow the van until it broke down, so we knew which garage to go to. After that, all we had to do was visit the garage on some pretext or other, get hold of the keys and then have duplicates made.

I have to admit that I was nervous about the whole thing because even with the best of planning there were still a lot of things that could go wrong, but I was determined not to back out, not after we'd come this far. The good news was that by this time, Brenda was completely sold on the idea and if anything, was even more committed than I was.

The next stage was to sabotage the wages delivery truck. The following Sunday, at three o'clock in the morning, I climbed over the wall of the security firm with a gallon of oil under my arm. Brenda, who had driven me into town, was waiting in the car at a car park about half a mile away.

After that it was just a case of finding the right security van, pouring the oil into the petrol tank, then climbing out again. It all went like clockwork and I doubt I was on the security firm's premises for more than ten minutes all told.

I know I've made it all sound very simple and straightforward, but the truth is it really wasn't that difficult, though I have to admit that my heart was beating like a trip-hammer most of the time. What really amazed me was that given the fact that the company was in the security business, they really had no idea about how to protect their own premises.

I remember the look on Brenda's face when I got back to the car when it was all over. I'd never seen her that excited before. "Well?" she said.

"Smooth as silk," I said. "Smooth as silk."

The next morning – the Monday – I took a couple of hours off again and followed the security van on its rounds, but it didn't break down, though there seemed to be a lot of blue smoke coming out of the exhaust pipe. That was very disappointing, but I was determined not to be put off by what I described as a minor setback.

"I'm going to go back again tonight," I told Brenda.

I took a gallon of water with me the second time and I had no more trouble sabotaging the van the second time than I had the first.

The next day the wages van made its first delivery without any problems, but then it wouldn't start. Not long after, another security van came along to take away all the strongboxes, then a breakdown truck arrived to tow it away. After that, it was just a case of making sure I knew which garage they had gone to.

That afternoon after work, Brenda and I paid the garage a visit. While I spoke to the manager about having my car serviced, Brenda wandered around inside the workshop. I watched her drift over to where the security van was parked then I went inside the office and booked my car in for a service the next morning.

When I got back to my car, she was already waiting for me. "Easy as taking candy from a baby," she said, holding up the keys.

From the garage we went directly to a key cutter and got some copies made, then it was back home.

I have to admit that I didn't sleep very well that night. I kept worrying that someone would want to move the security van or something like that and then they'd discover the keys were missing. I mean, we'd already committed at least two serious offences and were planning to do something even worse. All of a sudden, what had seemed like a brilliant idea for such a long time was now completely different. This wasn't a game any more. It was serious. And soon there would be no going back.

In the end, I got up and made myself a cup of tea. I spent most of the night pacing around the kitchen, but Brenda slept like a baby.

We were back at the garage at seven o'clock the next morning. While I waited in a queue to book my car in, Brenda put the keys back in the security van. I thought she'd be stopped by one of the mechanics or something like that, but the whole thing went off without a hitch.

"When are we going to do it?" she asked, when we were walking down the road outside.

I suddenly felt very dizzy and light-headed. I had to sit down at a bus stop to get my breath back, but she didn't show any sympathy.

"Well?" she said, impatiently.

It was all I could do to keep my voice steady.

"Soon," I said.

"Soon when?"

She was a typical woman when she got a bee in her bonnet: insistent, nagging. "Well?" she said when I didn't answer.

For a moment I couldn't think straight.

"Next week," I said finally. "A week on Friday."

I would have liked more time, but I could see Brenda wasn't going to wait.

"Good," she said, looking all pleased with herself. "Good."

EIGHT

"WE HAVE TO GO OVER THE PLAN, even down to the smallest detail,"
I said that night.

We were in my flat, in the kitchen where we'd just eaten supper. We
didn't go to my place very often because Brenda said it was uncomfortable, but her flatmate was at home and we needed somewhere quiet.

Brenda, who was washing up, nodded, very serious.

"We are now moving into Stage Two," I said, "which is stealing the
wages van, and there are a number of issues we have to consider. For
example, both of us will have to be absent from work on the morning
we hijack the van. How are we going to explain that?"

She picked up a plate from the draining board, began drying it with
a dishcloth.

"Maybe we won't have to. No one really knows we're a couple so
why should anyone be suspicious if we're both away from work at the
same time." After a pause, she added, "Anyway, if worst comes to worst
we can provide alibis for each other."

I'm not one to dwell on negative thoughts.

"We have to make sure it won't come to that," I said sharply. That's
why we're not going to leave anything to chance."

She turned to stare at me, putting the pressure on. "That's why you
have to make sure nothing goes wrong, Matthew," she said.

On the Friday morning we hijacked the wages van, I got up early and
put the false number plates on my car that I'd had made the week
before, then I phoned Mrs Williams in personnel and said I had a flat
tyre. You could tell she thought I was skiving off from the way she said,
"Just be as quick as you can," but I didn't take any notice.

Brenda phoned Jenny Martin and said she'd got a stomach bug.
Then she phoned the doctor to make an appointment.

At eight o'clock we met at the local shopping centre and the truth is

I didn't recognise Brenda when she first came up to me. (We'd slept at our own places the night before.) She was wearing one of my old suits, which she'd altered herself, plus a wig, false beard and moustache and was carrying a brown sports bag containing some ordinary clothes that she was going to need when it was all over. Of course I knew she was going to be disguised as a man, but she looked completely different to what I'd expected. I don't think her own mother would have known her that morning.

I had on baggy jeans, a lumberjack shirt, a long wig and a droopy moustache. It was what we called my hippie ensemble.

It would have been funny, the two of us dressed up like we were going to a fancy dress party, if everything hadn't been so serious, I mean.

And we did get one or two funny looks when we were walking to my car, but I honestly think most people didn't notice anything out of the ordinary.

I'd felt nervous all morning, but it wasn't until I got back into the car that I suddenly felt abject panic sweep over me. My hands were shaking. It was like I was being swept down a raging river, out of control and helpless.

"Are you sure you want to go through with this?" I asked, when I'd got the engine going.

Brenda, who up to that point hadn't seemed in the slightest concerned, turned to stare at me. "You're not trying to back out now, are you?" she said.

"No, of course not. I just want to make sure, that's all."

She gave me a long suspicious look before she turned away. "That's alright then."

She waved her hands in the air, urging me to move off. "We'd better get going," she said.

We left the shopping centre, drove across town to the security firm and parked down the road, out of sight of the front gates. It was a grey day. Everywhere was damp and the sky was full of low cloud. When the wages truck left the yard, we were following it, neither of us talking.

At the first stop after collecting the money, the driver stayed inside the vehicle while his assistant got out and handed over a strongbox to a security man who was waiting in the car park. Then they drove to Broads, which is where we were planning to carry out the robbery.

The wages truck parked outside Broads' main office block and both the driver and his mate got out, took another strongbox out of the side door and then headed for Reception.

I was on the move the moment they went inside the building, but I'd hardly taken two paces when they came out again.

When I got back in the car I was breathing so hard it looked like I'd just run a marathon.

"They didn't stay inside," I said.

At first, Brenda, who had already moved over to the driver's seat, didn't say anything.

"I think we have to cancel the whole thing and try again next week," I said.

She was pulling on a pair of gloves, looking at me like she thought I'd gone mad. "I think you need to get a grip on yourself, Matthew," she said very sharply and put the car into gear.

At the next stop, the wages van stopped just inside the factory gates and again the driver and his mate got out and carried a strongbox into the main building. I knew I had to spring into action, but I couldn't seem to move myself. It was like all the strength had gone out of my legs.

Brenda thumped me on the arm. "What are you waiting for?" she said, then a moment later, "Shit!"

She'd snatched up the keys and was on her way across the road before I had a chance to answer.

By the time I'd moved into the driving seat, I could see her getting into the wages van. Thirty seconds later, I was driving down the road behind her.

We drove to a piece of waste ground nearby, unloaded five strong boxes into the boot of my car and were on our way again almost before the alarm was raised.

Brenda changed into her ordinary clothes in the back of the car on the way to the doctor's surgery where she'd made an appointment that morning, then, after I'd dropped her off, I drove to a multi-storey car park where I put my proper number plates back on, and got ready for work myself. On my way to Thompsons, I dropped my spare tyre off at a garage to have it repaired – I'd driven a nail into the tyre the night before, to make it look authentic – and was back at my desk almost before anyone had missed me. I had absolutely no idea how much money I had sitting in the boot of my car that was parked downstairs in the yard.

The first hint that something was wrong was when I got a telephone call from the head of finance about an hour later. He had just been informed, he told me, that the company payroll, along with some other money had been hijacked that morning.

"What about the wages?" I said.

"The security people are going to deliver some more money, but it will be later."

He wanted to know if I would stay at my desk and work over lunchtime to make up the backlog. He sounded very grateful when I said that I'd be happy to do anything I could to help.

I saw the second security van arrive two hours later. It was a different van and a different driver and mate and they were very careful, the one staying next to the van looking around suspiciously all the time until the other returned from the wages office.

After they'd gone, the head of finance phoned me again. He told me that someone with keys to the van had stolen the wages payroll. "It sounds like an inside job to me," he said.

I made an effort to keep my voice steady when I asked him if he knew how much money had been stolen.

"About £300 000, I think," he said.

After I put the phone down, I walked to the canteen for something to do. I couldn't sit still and my hands were shaking again, I was so nervous. I had no idea what that amount of money looked like. Brenda, who by this time had got back from the doctor, was sitting at her desk typing. She didn't even look up when I walked past.

NINE

THAT NIGHT WE FORCED OPEN the strong boxes in the kitchen at my flat. We used a hammer and chisel that I'd bought at a hardware store on my way home from work that afternoon. I had to bash at the locks for nearly half an hour, using a blanket to deaden the noise, before I could get them all open. The total amount of money inside the five boxes came to £328 560, which was a lot more than we'd expected. After we'd counted the cash and it was lying in big piles all over the kitchen floor, we both stood back, staring down at all of it. We were actually speechless for a few moments; then we burst out laughing and did a little jig, kicking all the piles of notes into the air like demented loons.

After that, we gathered up all the money again and stuffed it into two holdalls, which I hid in the airing cupboard behind the geyser. Then we wiped down the strongboxes, to get rid of any fingerprints, and put them in the boot of my car. The next morning I got up before dawn, drove out into the country and dumped them in the river before heading back to work.

The robbery was big news, of course. In one of the papers a police spokesman was quoted as saying that the job had been carried out by a team of "skilled professionals". I have to tell you, it made me very proud to read that.

We weren't quite sure what to do with all the money because we knew we couldn't pay it into our bank accounts or anything like that, so in the end we decided that I would keep one holdall full of cash and Brenda would keep the other.

It was when we were driving over to Brenda's place after we'd split up the money, that she dropped her bombshell.

"I quite fancy going on a bit of a shopping spree this weekend," she said very casual-like. "Maybe get a nice tennis bracelet. Nothing ostentatious, mind you, just something classy."

Of course, I saw red straight away. As far as I was concerned, we'd already agreed we couldn't spend any of the money for a long time, not until we knew it was absolutely safe.

"Don't be stupid," I said.

"Then why did we steal the money in the first place if we aren't going to spend it?" she asked, glaring at me. I could see that she wanted to argue the point.

"We are going to spend it," I said, "but not now, not until it's safe."

"And when's that going to be?"

"I don't know."

She let out a sigh, making a big show of controlling her temper.

"What I want to know is why you make all the decisions," she said.

I could see she was very angry, so I told her to calm down. Then I reminded her that we'd agreed not to touch the money for at least three months so as not to draw attention to ourselves. Apart from anything else, I said, we didn't know if any of the notes were traceable.

"I'm not talking about buying a fucking jumbo jet, I'm talking about a fucking bracelet!" she shouted.

Very quietly, I asked her to keep her voice down. Then I waited until she looked like she'd got her temper tantrum under control.

"It's the principle that matters," I said finally.

That's when she put her fingers down her throat, pretending to make herself sick.

"Fuck the principle," she said, when she stopped making gagging noises.

When I said that I didn't think it was very ladylike to use that kind of language she started to laugh. "We're not talking about me being a fucking lady," she said, very calm and collected.

I knew she'd only used the "eff" word for effect this time, so I didn't rise to the bait.

"Yes, you're right," I agreed. "We're talking about not getting caught."

I think that took the wind out of her sails because she dropped the subject, but I don't think she was very happy about it.

For a couple of days, the robbery was front-page news in all the papers and there was even a police photo-fit picture of the hijacker, who was described as a "slim, bearded man of medium height". Eventually the story drifted to page two then a week later, no one was talking about it any more.

There were changes at work though. A new set of security guards was in charge of the wages delivery and there were no more leisurely cups of tea for them in the canteen. We also heard that the police were grilling the security firm's employees, mainly because a duplicate set of keys had been used in the heist, which, we heard, indicated an "inside" job.

The rumours were that the police didn't have much to go on, but even if that was true, I knew we weren't out of the woods yet, so I stressed to Brenda that there was no reason for complacency.

Three days after the robbery, a team of detectives descended on Thompsons to conduct some interviews. Although I was very worried at the time, now that I look back on things I don't believe the fact that Brenda and I were absent from work when the robbery took place was seen as particularly significant. To begin with, there were seventeen other members of staff also off the premises at the time in question, taking into account those who were on holiday and sick leave and the sales reps and so on. And I don't think the "skilled professionals" the police were looking for included a secretary and a wages clerk. How many people were missing from work at the time of the robbery at all the other firms affected, I never found out.

Detective Constable Bennett, the police officer who interviewed me, was a big, pot-bellied man who arrived in my office unannounced on the Wednesday morning after the robbery.

"I need to ask you some questions," he said, sitting down in front of my desk.

He'd taken me by surprise and that made me nervous, but I think I covered it up well by fussing over some sheets of paper, which I put away in a filing cabinet. By the time I sat down, I was composed and ready.

He asked some questions about where I was and what I was doing at the time of the robbery. I explained that I'd arrived late for work that morning because of a puncture, which I'd had repaired at a local garage. I gave him the name and address of the garage in question and even showed him the receipt for the repair, which he took away with him, though he didn't seem particularly interested.

As he was leaving I asked him if the police had any leads to go on. He didn't say much but I got the impression that they were pretty much stumped by the whole thing. When I remarked that they might catch the thieves when they started spending the money, he started to laugh.

"You've been watching too many police dramas, Mr Woodgate," he said, which I took to mean that the notes weren't traceable.

No one interviewed Brenda and we never heard anything else about the robbery after that, but as you can imagine, the first couple of weeks were very tense. I was confident, of course, but despite the fact that I'd tried to plan everything right down to the smallest detail, there was no anticipating the unexpected. That was something I kept trying to impress on Brenda, who didn't seem to think anything could possibly go wrong if we hadn't been arrested over the first weekend. I'm not a pessimist by nature, but I have to confess that those first few weeks were a difficult time for me.

After a month it became obvious to everyone that the police weren't making any progress with their investigation. One of the things in our favour, I suspect, was the fact that Thompsons wasn't the only company affected by the robbery. There were at least three other firms involved, which must have meant that the list of possible "inside" suspects was considerable to say the least. In my opinion that was one of the main reasons why we got away with it with so easily.

We didn't spend a penny of the money for over two months and when we did start to splash out a bit, we were very careful. The first time we went on a shopping spree, for example, we drove to Liverpool. That day we spent nearly a thousand pounds. We bought a new toaster and a camera for me, and a pair of gold earrings and a video recorder for Brenda.

We also both wore our disguises again, which may seem extreme, but I think it was necessary. Brenda wasn't keen on the idea of course, of us disguising ourselves, I mean, and was all for throwing caution to the wind and going as ourselves, but I insisted on "Minimum Safety Standards", as I called them. As I pointed out to her, one can never be too careful with all the security cameras that shops have nowadays.

Strange as it may seem, the fact that I suddenly had a lot more money than before wasn't all that important, once I got used to the idea. As far as I was concerned, just knowing it was there and that we'd outwitted the forces of law and order, so to speak, was the most important thing, though I don't think the same could be said for Brenda. Easy come, easy go, she used to say and I've no doubt she'd have spent the whole lot in the first month, given half the chance. But then she could be very headstrong and impetuous at times, could Brenda. I also noticed that she'd become a lot more assertive and self-assured after the robbery. To be truthful, I didn't like her always answering me back like she started to do, but there wasn't a lot I could do about it, not without a stand-up fight, that is.

Mind you, in her defence, it was a very unsettling time for us both. I think part of the problem was that it was difficult to go back to an ordinary nine-to-five existence after all the excitement of the robbery and its build-up. That's why we soon started talking about doing another job, to get the adrenalin rush again, as Brenda called it.

At first we talked about another robbery, a bank or building society, that sort of thing, but the truth was that neither of us was very enthusiastic about the idea. I think we both knew that we'd been lucky the first time. Also, doing a "proper" bank robbery, as I called it, was likely to be a lot more difficult, a different kettle of fish entirely. Of course, I could say that the fear of getting caught was half the fun, but I had no intention of doing something that was just plain reckless and ending up in prison for twenty years just for a bit of excitement.

TEN

IT WAS BRENDA WHO CAME UP with the idea of kidnapping someone. I think she got the inspiration while watching the news on TV. There was a story about some Nigerians who had kidnapped a Scandinavian business-man in South Africa. It was something to do with money laundering. Anyway, according to the news report the businessman was taken from his hotel room in Johannesburg, then his family started getting ransom notes for a million dollars. After they'd paid over the money, Interpol got involved and saved the businessman's life, though the kidnappers got away with the cash.

We were at Brenda's flat and I'd been making cocoa in the kitchen while the news was on. When I walked back into the lounge she had a big grin on her face, so I knew something was potting.

"I think we should kidnap someone," she said quite casually, like what she was suggesting was the most normal thing in the world.

"I don't think that's a very good idea," I said, putting the cups down. I didn't think she was serious.

She just nodded then took a drink, all the time keeping her eyes on me over the rim of her cup.

"Why not?" she said after a pause.

"Because kidnappers get caught."

"Not all of them."

"No, not all, but most of them. Anyway, whom would we kidnap?"

"I don't know."

I was about to say, exactly my point, but she didn't give me a chance.

"I don't think that's important," she said quickly. "Not now anyway. What's important is deciding whether or not to do it."

"Kidnapping is difficult and dangerous," I said.

She was staring at me and nodding, agreeing with me. "I'm not saying there isn't a risk, Matthew, just that it's something we should think about."

That's when I realised she was earnest.

"If we could kidnap Pavarotti or Salman Rushdie or someone like that," I said, "we could get a good ransom, but we can't. Famous people like that have bodyguards to protect them."

What I was really trying to say was that I thought the whole idea was stupid, but I didn't want to say that, not in so many words, anyway, but she didn't want to listen because a moment later, she said, "We don't need someone that well-known, just a businessman or someone with money. It doesn't have to be anyone famous."

I picked up my mug of cocoa and took a drink instead of answering. I knew I had to nip the idea in the bud, but I wasn't quite sure how.

"Kidnapping someone isn't that easy, Brenda," I said.

I pretended to look at the TV, like I thought she was joking or something, but out of the corner of my eye I saw her give me a sharp look, a sneer almost, though I didn't say anything. By that time, you see, I knew Brenda well enough to know that although she'd get irritated and impatient if she couldn't get her own way, sooner or later she'd let things drop if I just ignored her.

I thought that was the end of the matter until she brought up the subject again about a week later. This time we were at work and she was in my office, waiting for me to sign a letter she'd typed.

"If we do things right we could kidnap someone and get away with it without too much risk," she whispered.

I carried on reading the letter. "I don't think this is the right time or place to discuss the matter," I answered, not looking up.

"We'd have the element of surprise," she persisted. "The person we kidnapped wouldn't have a clue what was happening until it was too late."

I thought she was being ridiculous. Couldn't she see I was totally against the idea? That's when I nearly lost my temper.

"So how do we get the cash?" I asked very cynical-like. "Maybe we could say, Meet me outside Sainsbury's in the High Street, or, if you don't like that idea, why don't we just drive straight to the police station and give ourselves up and save everyone a lot of trouble."

I half expected some smart-aleck answer, but she surprised me by just ignoring the sarcasm, keeping very calm

"I've thought about that," she said quietly. "We'd have to make sure the person bringing us the cash was always moving from place to place. That way we could suddenly intercept them and take the money without warning. We could get away before anyone had a chance to stop us."

"Easier said than done," I said.

"Yes, I know. But it's not impossible, is it?"

She sounded very eager and she still hadn't raised her voice or got agitated, which was a new Brenda, a Brenda I'd never seen before.

"No," I said, "it's not impossible – but it's impractical. Kidnapping someone only happens in the films. In the real world there are just too many problems involved."

That's when she finally reacted, like I'd been expecting her to do all along.

"I can't believe I'm hearing this," she said incredulously. "You're the one who came up with the idea of robbing the security van and that went off as smooth as clockwork. When we did that we were up against a whole security company. This time, we'd only be up against one person."

"No, that's not true. We'd be up against the whole police force. Anyway, I didn't say we couldn't kidnap someone. That's easy. What I don't think we can do is get away with it."

"We got away with the hijacking, didn't we?"

"Yes," I said, "but that was different."

"No, it isn't. If we plan carefully I don't see any reason why we can't get away with a kidnapping too."

"We might have to keep the victim locked away for days or weeks even," I said.

"So?"

I couldn't believe she didn't see that as a problem. But as I said earlier, Brenda has a tendency to act first and think afterwards, to gloss over the details that don't quite fit in with her plan.

"I don't think I can manage the job of full-time jailer as well as running the finance department," I said.

"But kidnapping's not completely out of the question, is it?" she said.

"No," I said, "it's not completely out of the question."

She smiled, then picked up the letter from my desk.

"We can make a lot of money," she whispered, like this was some kind of inducement.

"We've already got a lot of money," I reminded her.

"Then we can have some fun. If I don't get some excitement soon, I'll go off my head."

"I need more time to think," I said. "I don't want to talk about it here."

"Where then?"

"At home."

She gave me a big grin then flounced out of my office, waving the letter like she'd just won a glorious victory.

"What's up with you today?" I heard one of the other girls call out to her.

"Can't a girl just be happy?" Brenda asked.

I now know that Brenda started looking for someone local to kidnap the day after the conversation in my office. I was furious when I found out what she'd been up to, but I didn't say anything, which was a mistake, I suppose, but this was before I really got involved, when I still thought of the idea as nothing more than an interesting mental exercise. To be honest, what I expected to happen was that she'd do a bit of investigating, realise the difficulties involved and then give up the idea without me having to say a word. That didn't happen, of course, but how was I to know that at the time?

Given the terrible way things turned out in the end, and knowing what I know now, I sometimes wonder if she didn't have the whole thing planned all along.

It was about a week later that Brenda came up with a name. At the time we were in her flat watching a video called Platoon, which was about the Vietnam War. We'd paused the film so that Brenda could make some sandwiches. When she came out of the kitchen and put the tray down on the coffee table she said, "I know who we can kidnap."

I was tempted to laugh. "You're like a dog with a bone," I said, then when I saw the look she was giving me, I sighed, rolling my eyes at the ceiling, making a big thing out of it.

"Go on," I said.

She went to her bag and took out a copy of the local paper. First, she folded it back at the society section then smoothed it out on the table, pushing it towards me.

"Her," she said, pointing.

She'd drawn a red circle around a picture showing a group of young people at an art gallery opening. The girl she had picked out was hanging onto the arm of a tall good-looking man with dark swept-back hair. She was holding up a glass of wine, like she was saluting the camera. Her face was vaguely familiar, but I couldn't put a name to it.

"Her name's Sarah Fitzgibbon. Her father's a rich businessman."

The first thing that struck me was that Sarah Fitzgibbon was a beautiful young woman. She had shoulder-length blond hair parted in the middle and was wearing a short black dress, low cut at the front, to show off her figure. I could tell straightaway from the grin on her face that she had that sort of easy self-confidence – arrogance some would call it – that was as natural as breathing to people of her type. The rich and the well bred, I mean. The silver-spoon-in-the-mouth brigade, the sort of people who always look down on you because you aren't brought up their way, the sort of people I instinctively despised.

"She'd be easy to kidnap," Brenda said. "The rich aren't like us, they think that everything's been arranged for their benefit."

Yes, that's true, I thought, but I didn't say anything. I couldn't take my eyes off the picture. Discussing the idea of carrying out a kidnapping had been interesting in an abstract kind of way, but now all of a sudden we were talking about a real person.

"Well?" she said.

"We don't know anything about her," I answered. "She might have half a dozen big bodyguards watching her every move."

"Yes, that's true – and if she has, then we choose someone else, don't we?"

When I didn't say anything, she carried on. "But unless we find out something about her, we can't do anything, can we?"

I didn't answer, not for a long time anyway.

"How much would you expect as a ransom," I asked finally.

"I don't know. Half a million pounds sounds a nice round figure to me. What do you think?"

"That's a lot of money."

"It's all relative. Five hundred thousand to one person is the same as five hundred to someone else."

"Not to me it isn't," I said.

"We're not talking about kidnapping you, Matthew," she whispered and blew air into my ear.

The very next day Brenda came up with yet another surprise.

"I'm thinking of giving up my job so I can devote all of my time to putting a plan together," she said. "What do you think?"

"I think you're getting carried away," I said.

She looked down. When she looked up again, she said, "I knew you'd say that," sounding all high and mighty.

I was seething. "A stupid idea is a stupid idea," I told her.

The day after that she asked me if I knew where she could get some chloroform from.

By this time I was losing my patience with her.

"You're becoming completely ridiculous," I said.

The strange thing is, the more I poured cold water on her plans, the more determined she seemed to become. It was quite encouraging in a sense, seeing her so eager and enthusiastic, I mean, but I started to think that if I didn't take her more seriously and get more actively involved, she was likely to do something impetuous and get us both into trouble. That's how I came to sit her down at my place, to explain how things needed to be done.

We were in the lounge. I'd bought us a fish and chip supper, which we'd eaten out of the paper.

"I think you need to slow down, Brenda," I said. "Kidnapping someone is not the sort of thing you just rush into."

I saw her eyes go glittery and she had her lips pressed together. I knew she was furious, but that couldn't be helped. "You're going about this in completely the wrong way," I said.

"Oh, and you know better, do you?" she sneered.

"Yes, I do."

I think she'd assumed that just because she'd come up with the original idea this had given her some kind of special privilege. That's why I felt it necessary to remind her just who was in charge.

"From now on we do things my way", I said.

For a long moment she didn't say anything. I thought she was going to start arguing the point, but instead she just shrugged and said, "Okay," like it was no big deal.

She could be very unpredictable at times.

Eleven

"THE FIRST THING WE HAVE to do is find out a lot more about your Ms Fitzgibbon," I said to Brenda the next day.

She nodded, very solemn. "Yes, you're right."

I thought she'd agreed too easily. That's why I warned her that I still wasn't entirely sold on the kidnapping idea.

"And even if we do decide to abduct someone, your Ms Fitzgibbon may not be the kind of person we're looking for," I added.

"Then I think I'd better look into the matter, don't you, Matthew?" she said.

Of course, I wasn't very optimistic, what with her being so scatter-brained, which is why I was so surprised a week later when she presented me with a whole file of clippings that she'd photocopied at the local library.

I was quite alarmed when I saw how much work she'd done.

"You didn't draw attention to yourself, did you?" I asked.

The last thing I wanted was to kidnap someone and then end up being picked out in a police identity parade by some nosy librarian who'd seen what Brenda was up to.

The moment I said that she snatched the file back and I saw her face change, go dark with rage, I mean, I wasn't going to tolerate any defiance, not when there was so much at stake.

"Don't start getting your temper up with me," I warned.

"What kind of fool do you take me for?" she shouted.

After I'd told her to keep her voice down, I calmly explained that I didn't take her for a fool, but that I needed to be certain that things were being done right. She turned her back on me and wouldn't speak for ten minutes. But in the end she calmed down and showed me what she'd got from the library.

I have to admit, the more I found out about Sarah Fitzgibbon, the more I liked her. Not as a person, of course, because I could tell she thought too much of herself, rather as someone to take down a peg or two. I hate snobs, you see: her sort of people, the sort of people who want to see themselves in the newspapers all the time like they're celebrities, when all they've really done is get themselves born rich and beautiful.

In most of the newspaper reports – Our Sarah – as Brenda had started calling her, was either doing something outrageous, like driving her sports car at 100 miles an hour in a built-up area, or causing trouble by getting drunk or throwing things around and shouting. She was your typical spoilt little rich girl.

In one article, for example, she'd been arrested after she and her boyfriend left a nightclub, obviously the worse for drink. A policeman stopped her from getting into her car, which is when the reporter who was at the scene said she became abusive, though she denied it. The police officer said she called him a "fascist pig", then tried to drive away, which is why he'd had to arrest her.

At the police station she was charged with drunken driving. After that, she phoned daddy, who arrived in the company of a high-powered lawyer. No doubt daddy was hoping to browbeat the local constabulary into submission, though without too much success it seems because when she went to court three weeks later, she had her driving licence revoked for 12 months and was given a £300 fine.

In a later edition, there was a picture of her on the steps of the Magistrates Court building after the court case. She was dressed in a short skirt, showing her legs off and had her hair piled up on top of her head, all wild and freaky. According to the reporter, she'd referred to the judge as an "old fart" who "had it in for her".

In another paper Brenda had fished out, she was sticking her tongue out to the law courts.

What daddy thought of Our Sarah's behaviour wasn't mentioned.

"It looks to me like she needs a good lesson in manners, Brenda," I said.

"Yes, that's what I think, too."

"From now on we'll have to be the soul of discretion," I said.

"Extra-specially careful, I mean because there are still a lot of questions we need to answer."

"Absolutely, Matthew," she said, "Absolutely."

The next day I made a few notes at work and when Brenda came into my office I slipped them into her hand. "We need to think about these," I whispered.

I'd written down six questions that we needed to answer before we went any further with the plan:

Where do we keep her?

How do we find out where she goes?

How do we kidnap her?

How much money do we ask for?

How exactly do we get the money?

When and where do we kidnap her?

Brenda took a quick look at the list then gave me a big smile. It was like I'd just given her a winning lottery ticket.

"So you're finally in now, are you?" she said.

"Yes, I'm in if we do things properly," I answered, which was the truth.

"Of course we'll do things properly, Matthew," she said all sweetness and light.

"One of the most important questions we have to answer is where are we going to keep Our Sarah while we wait for the ransom money to come through," I said to Brenda that night.

We'd taken a drive out into the country for a change and had stopped for a drink at a pub called the Hare & Hound. It was crowded and noisy but we'd managed to get a table to ourselves in the bar.

"I've thought about that," Brenda said. "We can't keep her at my place or yours and a hotel or guest house is out of the question too. That means we have to find somewhere else – a farmhouse or something like that would be perfect. Somewhere quiet and remote would be best."

She was very businesslike for a change. I couldn't help feeling I was witnessing a transformation.

"That may not be so easy," I said.

"I know," Brenda said briskly, "but there must be estate agents who keep lists of properties up for rent. All we have to do is choose the one we want."

I thought it would be a lot more difficult than that, but I decided to keep quiet about it.

"We have to be discreet," I said. "I don't just mean trying to keep our names a secret, what I'm talking about goes a lot further than that. Always being on our guard, I mean. No one must have any idea what we're up to."

"Alright, then maybe we can pay cash when we rent a place?" she said, giving me one of her sharp looks. "That way there's no record."

I thought she was missing the point, that we had to be careful about everything we did, not just about finding somewhere to keep our victim, but I didn't say so because I didn't want her to fly off into one of her rages. I knew from experience that when I wanted her to do something, it was best to move slow and easy, to give her a lot of little nudges, so to speak, rather than one big shove.

"First, we find out where she lives and what her routine is. We can start to look for her by going to some nightclubs. It'll be hit or miss in the beginning, but being as she likes the high life, I can't see any reason why we shouldn't be able to track her down sooner or later."

She was very enthusiastic, animated almost.

"You've given this a lot of thought, haven't you?" I said, and I could see that she was pleased.

"I've tried to be efficient and organised like you," she answered. She paused then, but I could see there was something else on her mind.

"I think we need a gun," she said, then seeing the look on my face. "I don't mean a real one, silly, I mean a toy. We can buy one at a toyshop. I checked it out, something that's life-like. To scare her. Then we'd look really threatening and the girl wouldn't know the difference, not at first anyway. It's what some bank robbers use," she added.

I hadn't even considered a gun, because I knew I couldn't get hold of one, but a toy one might be just the thing we needed.

After that we had a long debate about how much ransom money we should ask for. In the end we settled for the amount Brenda had mentioned in the first place – half a million pounds.

We also talked about how we could actually get hold of the money, but we didn't come up with a concrete plan of action, although we agreed that the thing we had to do was make the person delivering the money run from place to place. That way we'd be able to keep them on the wrong foot and confuse anyone who was trying to follow.

"There's a lot of detail still to work out," I said, "but the first thing we need to do is to sort out somewhere to keep the victim locked up."

"We can start looking on Saturday," Brenda said.

That weekend we took a drive out into the country to visit a couple of estate agents, to start the ball rolling, so to speak. I explained that we were looking to rent a farmhouse or a smallholding in the area, somewhere nice and quiet out of the city, somewhere to stretch our legs.

The first agent we visited specialised in residential property so wasn't much help, but the second one actually took us to see a couple of places that morning. The second cottage we saw would have been perfect for our needs except that it was too near to the main farmhouse. That was disappointing, of course, but we still came home elated because we could see that getting the sort of place we wanted wasn't out of the question, it was just a case of trying a bit harder and possibly widening our search a bit.

It took us another month to find the place we were looking for. After our first effort we wised up and got the names of some estate agents that specialised in rural properties from the Estate Agents Board. Then we made some phone calls and started setting up appointments. After that it was just a case of going to see different places until we found what we were looking for.

The place we finally rented was a shepherd's cottage, which was about half an hour's drive out of town. The house itself was a low, squat, granite-walled building with a roof of grey slate. Next to it was a small barn with big double doors that the estate agent said had originally been intended for storing bales of hay, but which was now used as a garage. The two buildings had been sited on a riverbank, behind a copse of trees, which meant they were hidden from the road, which we considered a distinct advantage. The main farmhouse where the owner of the property lived was over two miles away.

Inside the cottage there was a big, furnished living room-cum-kitchen with an open fireplace and two bedrooms off the lounge area, both with stout wooden doors. But what made it special was the cellar: a giant cavern of a room that ran almost the entire length of the house.

The farmer who owned the place had done the house out from top to bottom and he'd turned the cellar into a kind of master bedroom with a bathroom en-suite, though why anyone would want to sleep underground was beyond me. The estate agent said that the owner had expected to rent it out without too much trouble, but we were only the second couple to show any interest in the six months it had been on the market. For most people the place was just too remote, she said.

We paid cash for twelve months in advance that morning, with an option to extend the lease for a further six months if required and everyone was very happy. We didn't have to sign any papers or fill in any forms and the farmer didn't have to declare anything for tax. Money talks, as they say and the last thing the owner was going to do was look a gift horse in the mouth.

So we had our hideaway. Now we were ready for step two: planning the kidnapping.

TWELVE

BRENDA BECAME EVEN MORE determined after we rented the farmhouse. The following week she went back to the library every evening after work, this time to look through a whole year's back issues of the local newspaper. That's how she found out where Our Sarah's parents lived. We had looked in the telephone book but their name wasn't listed, presumably because it was ex-directory. In one article about a new shopping centre being built by Fitzgibbon Construction, there was the name of the street where "local socialites" Mr and Mrs Reginald Fitzgibbon lived and even a picture of their house, so we knew that finding the place wasn't going to be difficult.

At that time we didn't know if Our Sarah still lived with her parents, though we doubted it. Even so, we thought it was important to know where the parents lived. It was the kind of information that might just prove valuable sometime in the future. It also made us feel we were taking charge, us starting to know a lot about them and them knowing nothing about us, I mean.

That weekend, the one after the week Brenda had spent in the library, we went to look for the house where Our Sarah's mother and father lived. After we'd found the place, which turned out to be a lot easier than we expected, we parked outside the front gate for a couple of minutes while we pretended to look at a street map, then drove away. We didn't want to stay any longer for fear of drawing attention to ourselves. Of course, knowing where the parents lived didn't really help us find the daughter, but it did make us feel that we were making progress with our plans.

It was coincidence I suppose, but that same night there was an article in the Sunday paper about the "gala opening" of a new "supper club" called Rugs, the following Wednesday night.

Brenda became excited the moment she read the story. "That's just the sort of thing Our Sarah's likely to go to," she said.

What she meant was that we should go too.

"I can't see the point of paying good money to be deafened and jostled by a bunch of strangers for most of the night," I said.

What I really wanted to say was that I thought she was in too much of a hurry, that she needed to slow down a bit, to catch her breath, so to speak, but I didn't want to say so because I knew it wouldn't go down too well.

"This is not about you, it's about her!" she answered all snappy. Then, a moment later, "You know what your trouble is, Matthew? You don't know how to enjoy yourself."

"So what's enjoyable about mixing with the so-called beautiful people?" I asked. "All they do is make nuisances of themselves."

Brenda gave a big sigh and held her head in her hands like she couldn't believe what she was hearing.

"Didn't you hear what I said? This is about her, not you!"

When I didn't say anything, she threw her head back and rolled her eyes at the ceiling, very melodramatic-like.

"Sometimes you can be a royal pain in the arse, Matthew, you know that, don't you? Just because you think such and such doesn't necessarily mean it's right. Other people have opinions too, you know."

I gave her a sharp look to let her know that I didn't take kindly to her comments, but she just started beating her fists against her face like a mad person.

"Look, if it's that important to you, we'll go along," I said.

That's when she made a big show of dropping her head forward, gasping and exhausted.

"You know how when there's a fire and someone throws a blanket over it to put it out?" she said. "Well that's what you can do to a good time – stifle it."

"Yes, you're right," I said all cynical.

"I know I am," she said. "That's just the trouble, I know I am."

I didn't like her attitude or the way she spoke to me, but I didn't say anything because I wasn't in the mood to watch her throw another tantrum. Now I know that if I'd put my foot down a bit more, things might have all turned out differently, but like I said earlier: it's always easy to be wise after the event.

The upshot of all this is that Brenda got her way. That Wednesday night we went along to the "grand opening" of the new nightclub. The rest, as they say, is history.

Rugs turned out to be a converted carpet factory on the edge of an industrial estate: a large two-storey building of glass and steel, surrounded by a chain link fence. In front of the double-doors of the main entrance there was a small lawn, a flowerbed and a "VIP" parking area for about half a dozen cars and around the back, next to the loading bays, a much bigger car park for "Visitors".

When we got there at eight o'clock the place was buzzing and the road outside was already chock-a-block with cars. Eventually, we managed to get a space in the car park, but by the time we got to the front entrance there were already a lot of people waiting, which meant we had to queue for another hour before we could get in.

As I said to Brenda, I thought the new owners had done everything on the cheap. They'd turned the factory downstairs into an enormous dance floor by taking out all the machinery and blacking up the windows and they'd done a similar thing upstairs, this time by knocking out all the offices to make one big bar and restaurant.

Despite the noise, we stayed downstairs most of the time because that was where we'd be most inconspicuous. After about an hour of being jostled, we managed to get a couple of seats at a table next to the dance floor. But even sitting down it was very unpleasant, what with the thump-thump-thump of the music and all the people pushing and shoving, like Dante's Inferno, as I described it.

I have to say though that Brenda seemed to be enjoying herself. At one point she even wanted to dance, but I wouldn't hear of it. "We're here to work, not to enjoy ourselves," I said, which made her shake her head like she couldn't believe what she was hearing, but I didn't take any notice.

At one o'clock in the morning, after four hours of complete misery, we decided to go home, which was when Our Sarah and her boyfriend – the one from the newspaper – drove up in a red sports car, just as we were walking back to our car. I was all for calling it a night and trying again some other time, but Brenda wouldn't hear of it.

"We can't miss a chance like this," she said, all excited.

"If we wait for them to come out again we could be here for hours," I complained.

A minute before Brenda had been out of sorts, now she was suddenly willing and eager. "I know," she answered, which was when I realised it was no use arguing the point, so we got in the car, moved it to a spot where we could keep an eye on the main entrance, then made ourselves as comfortable as we could and settled down to wait.

They came out again four hours later, and it was obvious from the way Our Sarah staggered out of the building, falling over her feet that she was a lot worse for drink than when she went in. Her boyfriend had his arm around her waist, holding her up, though she didn't seem too keen on the idea if the way she kept trying to push him away was anything to go by. When they got near their car she tripped over and dropped her car keys and he bent down to pick them up, which is when she shoved him away, almost falling over herself in the process. Even from where we were sitting we heard her call him an effing bastard.

Brenda made an angry noise and I heard her say, "Bitch!" under her breath.

After a lot of shouting and arguing, the boyfriend managed to get the car keys off her and get her into the passenger seat, but it was obvious from the way she was waving her arms around that she was still going on at him even after he'd got the engine started and was pulling out of the car park.

"She's not a very nice girl," I said, joking almost, but Brenda's eyes were blazing.

"Drunken cow!" she hissed.

I hadn't expected to hear such venom in her voice.

"She just doesn't know any better," I said.

That's when Brenda looked at me. "I hate her," she said quietly.

They drove down through the town and just before Queen's Bridge turned into a narrow "For Residents Only" cul-de-sac named Boatman Mews. Instead of following them, though, we carried on along the main road and turned into a car park next to a small picnic site on the other side of the river.

They stopped outside the middle house in a row of eight, grey-stoned terraced cottages. It was a very picturesque street, the kind of area that estate agents like to describe as "quaint and attractive", which is another way of saying "expensive". Brenda, who seemed to know something about the area, said that the houses were over a hundred years old and had originally been built as fisherman's cottages, but that they'd recently been done up. Now they were very expensive. "The story was in all the papers," she said.

"I must have missed that particular article," I said, though I think the sarcasm was wasted.

We watched the boyfriend get out of the car, go around to the passenger side and help Our Sarah stagger up to the front door. She was so drunk she was falling over her feet and he was trying to help her, but she kept shrugging him off, wrenching her arm free every time he put a hand on her. When she finally got the front door open she turned and said something to him then pushed him away. I expected him to do something, try to force his way into the house or argue the point, but he just got back in the car and drove off. She'd already gone inside the house and switched the porch light off before he'd even got the engine started.

"Fucking wimp," Brenda said, meaning the boyfriend.

After he'd gone, we waited fifteen minutes then walked back over the bridge and took a quick stroll past her front door to make a note of the number. Then we walked to the end of the block. Behind the houses there was a narrow service road and a row of eight garages.

After that we went home tired but in good spirits. We now had a target, we knew where she lived and we had a place to keep her locked up while we negotiated a ransom. An added bonus we hadn't anticipated was that Our Sarah lived opposite a small riverside park, which meant we could occasionally take a stroll there and watch her house without arousing anyone's attention. It was almost too perfect, but as I said to Brenda, that was no reason for complacency.

Things were progressing a lot better than I'd anticipated but that's not to say there weren't any problems. A few days later, for example, I had to give Brenda a talking to. That was after I overheard her being told off by Jenny Martin because she hadn't typed a letter she was supposed to. That night when we got home, I gave her a piece of my mind.

"I'm very disappointed with you, Brenda," I said. "Don't you realise that we have to be above reproach? That we can't afford to draw any attention to ourselves?"

"It's not my fault!" she said, looking very heated, then went on to give me a long story about her being put-upon by the other girls, but I didn't let that sway me.

"We have to be perfect employees," I said.

"It's just so boring!" she said, as if that excused everything.

"Yes, of course it's boring," I said, "but we have to keep up appearances. We have to blend in with the woodwork, that way no one's going to suspect us of anything."

That's when she closed her eyes, slowly counting to ten, like she was doing everything she could to keep her patience in check.

"I think you're over-reacting," she said finally, giving me another of her condescending looks.

That made me angrier than ever. "If you don't make an effort to keep up appearances," I said, "I shall pull out of the whole thing."

I think she could tell from the look on my face that I was serious. That was when her expression changed, when she realised she'd overstepped the mark. Suddenly, she was all apologies.

"I'm sorry, Matthew, it's just that I get so bored at work. It won't happen again. I promise."

By that time I was livid, of course. "Just make sure you keep that promise," I said glaring at her. Then I walked away and went into the kitchen where I put the kettle on for a cup of tea, because I knew that if I didn't stop myself I'd end up saying something I regretted, about her being so hare-brained, I mean.

Five minutes later she came to apologise again. "Honestly, it won't happen again, Matthew," she repeated and after that she was as sweet as pie for the rest of the evening.

It just goes to show what I've always said: a woman sometimes needs a man's steadying influence to keep her on the straight and narrow.

By this time we were working on the finer details of the plan, talking about what instructions we'd give Our Sarah's father, where we'd make him go and that kind of thing. The Saturday after we found out where Our Sarah lived, for example, we spent the afternoon walking around the town centre, taking down the telephone numbers of the public phones we'd be using and timing how long it would take to get from place to place. As I said to Brenda, if we worked out the route properly one of us would be able to keep an eye on things all the time, to make sure there were no unexpected surprises – from the police, I meant. We also spent some time tying each other up, making sure we could do it right. That was because I insisted on everything being planned and organised like a military operation to make sure there were no complications.

About the last thing we did was get hold of a gun, which turned out to be a lot easier than I expected. Brenda and I bought a very authentic looking Smith & Wesson .45 automatic at a toyshop in the town centre. I told the shop assistant it was a birthday present for my nephew, not that she cared, of course. I admit that I don't know a lot about guns, but the one we bought looked very real to me. To be truthful, I'm surprised that toy guns haven't been banned.

THIRTEEN

IT WAS ABOUT TWO WEEKS after we'd followed Our Sarah home that we decided to take a picnic down to the park opposite where she lived. It had been a warm day and when we got there the sun was going down, the trees throwing long mottled shadows onto the river, making it a perfect evening. You have to remember that this was a smart part of town, and something of a local beauty spot what with the river and the park, which is why there were so many people about, walking their dogs, strolling along the tow path, and so on.

There were some concrete benches and tables next to the water and we used one of them for our picnic. Brenda had brought along a nice tablecloth and we looked, for all the world, like an ordinary courting couple simply spending some time together.

From where we were sitting, we had a perfect view of the house. We stayed until it had gone properly dark, which was around eight o'clock, but neither Our Sarah nor her boyfriend turned up. We were disappointed of course – especially Brenda, but I told her that this was the kind of thing we would have to get used to. As I said to her, the game wasn't going to play itself out exactly as we wanted. I think Brenda was more impatient than I was. I was used to taking my time, taking the long view, as I described it, but that didn't make much difference to her. For Brenda it had to be instant gratification or nothing.

We did the same thing two nights later. We took a picnic to the park and this time we saw Our Sarah arrive home at about seven o'clock. Her boyfriend was with her, the one that we had seen at the nightclub, but they seemed to have patched up their quarrel and were very lovey-dovey. When he opened the passenger door of his car for her, she almost leapt on him and gave him a big open mouth kiss. It was sickening the way she couldn't keep her hands off him. It was all she could do to get her key into the door.

Personally, I've always thought such public displays of affection are in extremely bad taste.

"They're making a complete spectacle of themselves," I said.

Brenda was staring so hard I don't think she heard me. She was like a statue. "They deserve whatever they get," she said very nastily, under her breath.

"Yes, you're right," I said.

"She's a selfish cow and he's a piece of shit!"

"You don't like him, do you? I asked.

I was trying to make a joke, but she took me seriously.

"I hate him. I hate him and I hate her!"

I'd never heard her sound so angry. It was almost like she was taking the whole thing personally, though to be truthful, I didn't think too much about it at the time. I just thought she was in one of her moods and was taking it out on Our Sarah and her boyfriend. After all, Our Sarah was nothing more than a spoilt little rich girl. Of course, I know now that I should have realised what was going on, but as I've said before, it's easy to be wise after the event, isn't it?

After they'd gone inside, Brenda calmed down again and we packed up and left, but at midnight we took another drive past the house. I wanted to know if her boyfriend would be staying the night, though I had no doubt that he would. And I was right. His car was parked with its wheels on the pavement outside the front door, just as I expected. And it was there at seven o'clock the next morning when I took a detour and drove past on my way to work.

"We have to make sure he's not around when we kidnap the girl," I said to Brenda. "We're likely to have enough complications as it is, without him causing any more." She agreed.

Eventually, we got all our ducks in a row, so to speak and it was time to act. We'd already made the decision that we were going to kidnap Our Sarah from her home and had stocked up the farmhouse where we were going to keep her. The only thing we still had to do was name the day.

I was quite anxious about the whole thing, but Brenda didn't seem to have any nerves at all, which I put down to the fact that she wasn't as cautious and calculating as I was. In fact, she seemed so eager I had to warn her not to get too excited, that we had to stay properly focused, as I put it.

Of course, it was even harder to concentrate at work when we were so close to carrying out our plan, but I insisted that everything had to appear normal on the outside. And Brenda was a good actress, I have to admit that, and I don't think anyone suspected that we were "an item" because we made sure that our relationship always appeared very cool and professional, distant even. We also made a point of going home in separate directions and would only meet at each other's apartments when it was safe.

"If this plan goes well," I said to Brenda one night, "we won't ever have to work again."

"We can go on a nice long holiday," she said.

"As long as we don't spend too much money or draw attention to ourselves," I reminded her.

We already had a small fortune from the wages heist and occasionally we'd get all the money out again, just to count it. The sight of all that cash was quite intoxicating and when we had the ransom money to add to it, I'd be able to go anywhere and do anything I wanted, not that I planned to buy a Ferrari or a private plane or anything like that after the kidnapping.

It was about this time that Brenda again returned to the subject of her handing in her notice at work.

As you can expect, I was dead against the idea.

"It will look very suspicious," I explained to her one night, "if you pack in your job one day and then go out and buy a Mercedes the next."

I could see she was irritated with me the minute I brought the subject up, but I didn't let that stop me.

"I don't want to buy a Merc, Matthew," she said sounding all high and mighty, "I just want to give up my job!"

"We have to take things nice and slow", I said. "We can both give up our jobs, but in good time, after the dust has settled."

She shrugged and that seemed to be the end of the matter, though I knew Brenda wasn't one to give up an idea once she'd set her mind on it.

Of course, I didn't tell her that I'd already written out my resignation, giving the firm a week's notice. I was waiting for the right time.

The week we planned to do the kidnapping we visited the park opposite Our Sarah's house three times. We always parked in different places so that we didn't become too conspicuous and as a precaution we started carrying the disguises with us, the same ones we had used for the wages heist – the lumberjack look for me, and the man's beard and suit for Brenda.

Twice we saw Our Sarah come out of her house, both times her boyfriend picked her up in his car and the next morning his car was parked outside, so it was obvious that he stayed over fairly often. That was the bad news. The good news was that he always seemed to park his car outside the front door when he visited, so all we had to do was kidnap her when his car wasn't there and he wouldn't get in the way.

The first Friday we set out to actually do the kidnapping both of us were very nervous. We drove to her house just as it was going dark and parked across the road, on the other side of the river. At about eight o'clock her boyfriend pulled up at the front door, she came out and they drove off together. I was disappointed because I knew he'd come back with her later on and stay the night, but we followed them all the same. They went to a fancy restaurant in the town centre and we had fish and chips in the car at the car park where they'd parked. They came out at ten and we were expecting them to go on to a nightclub or something like that, but they just drove back to her place and went inside. That was the end of that night. More or less the same thing happened the next night too, except they went to the cinema instead of a restaurant.

Brenda was champing at the bit, as you'd expect, but I explained to her that we had all the time in the world so it was important that we didn't make a move until everything was just right.

The plan was that when we knew Our Sarah was at home alone, the two of us would just knock on the front door on the pretext that our car had broken down and that we needed to use the telephone to phone the AA. When she answered, we'd shove her inside, tie her up, then Brenda would bring the car around the back and we'd bundle her into the boot.

FOURTEEN

IT WAS FRIDAY NIGHT two weeks later when we saw her come home and drive around the back of the house, at about seven-thirty, just as it was starting to get dark. We'd been parked across the road for about half an hour. Five minutes later a light went on over the porch. Brenda and I looked at each other. She was smiling; I was serious. "It's now or never," I said.

"Then it's now," Brenda said, and reached over into the back seat for her wig.

As soon as we were dressed, we walked over to the house and Brenda knocked on the front door.

Our Sarah answered about a minute later, after we'd had to knock twice more. She was scowling, clearly annoyed. "What do you want?" she said, not very politely.

"I'm very sorry to bother you," I said, speaking very softly, "but our car has broken down" – I glanced over my shoulder at this imaginary vehicle – "and we wondered if we could just telephone a garage."

She looked at me like I'd just crawled from under a stone. "No," she said.

"The public phone across the road is out of order," I said, before she had time to move away, but she wasn't interested, didn't bat an eyelid even. "Well, that's your hard luck, isn't it?"

When she went to close the door on us, I stepped forward and put my foot in the way.

There was a pause, like she couldn't quite work out what was happening. Then she found her tongue again.

"Piss off!" she said.

It was when she tried to shove my foot out of the way that I stuck the gun in her face.

"Get out of the way you fucking bitch," I said quietly.

I'm not sure if she even saw the gun. It was my voice that took her back because I don't think anyone had ever spoken to her quite like that before. I saw her face go all pale before she stepped back, then she put her hands in the air. We followed her inside. I took a quick look over my shoulder as Brenda was closing the door. All of a sudden there wasn't a soul about in the streets.

"The phone's over there," she said pointing at a hall side table. She still thought that all we wanted to do was use the telephone, the stupid idiot.

"Move," I said and she backed into the hallway.

"Who was that, Sarah?" a voice said.

When we went into the living room her boyfriend came out of the kitchen wiping his hands on his apron. Something smelled nice. Evidently he'd been cooking.

I suddenly felt panicked. This was exactly the situation we were trying to avoid, but we'd already gone too far to back out, so I pushed the gun at his face. Out of the corner of my eye I could see Brenda staring at him. I thought she was going to freeze up on me, but she found her voice even before I did.

"Get down on the floor, Mr Boyfriend," she whispered. Then, when he didn't react straight away, "Get down on the fucking floor!"

There was so much venom in her voice even I didn't recognise it. I think he was in shock, and when he still didn't move I turned and put the gun to his girlfriend's head. "Get on the floor with your hands on your head," I said, looking at him. I was very quiet and commanding this time, completely calm and in control.

They lay down side by side in front of the fireplace. She had one of those expensive gas fires, the ones with artificial coals and flickering flames. It was like everything else in the room – tasteful and expensive.

Brenda took a moment to glance into the kitchen, ran her fingers over a brass carriage clock on a side table. She was touching the furniture, admiring the décor.

"I have to say you've got a lovely place, Sarah," she said, sounding quite impressed. Sarah didn't answer her. She stared at me. "Please just take what you want and get out," a remark, which made Brenda give her an amused look, like she couldn't quite believe what she was hearing.

"But that's just what we're going to do, you stupid fucking bitch," she said, very matter-of-factly.

We'd agreed that I was going to do all the talking, because we thought her voice might give us away, so I gave Brenda a sharp look, which she ignored.

"Tie them up," she said.

"Please, you don't have to do that," the girl pleaded.

I pointed the gun at her head again and saw her flinch away from the sight. "You've been told to shut the fuck up," I whispered.

That was when Brenda stepped forward and without warning gave Our Sarah a kick in the ribs, putting all her strength in it, driving all the air out of her lungs, making her double up in pain.

I was too shocked to say anything.

"Next time you'll know that when you're told to do something you do it straight away, won't you, Sarah dear?" Brenda said sweetly, above the moans.

That was when the boyfriend rallied to her defence. "You don't have to do that," he said, making Brenda round on him.

"Not if she keeps very, very, very quiet, I won't," she warned, which seemed to do the trick because suddenly Our Sarah stopped most of the noise she was making.

That was when Brenda looked at her again.

"Isn't it incredible what a little bit of gentle persuasion can achieve," she said, shaking her head with amazement.

We'd both brought lengths of electric flex with us, so I passed the gun over to Brenda then bent down to tie the boyfriend's hands behind his back. After that was done, I felt a bit more relaxed so I took the gun back and left Brenda to deal with the girl.

That was when Our Sarah said something to her, when she was being tied up, I mean. I couldn't make out what it was, though it made Brenda giggle like a schoolgirl.

"You're a treasure, Sarah," she said grinning from ear to ear, "an absolute treasure."

When they were both tied up we put strips of masking tape over their mouths and pillowcases over their heads. The girl had started whimpering again, was hysterical almost, but I knew she wasn't going to be any trouble; it was the boyfriend I was worried about. He'd remained a lot calmer than I'd expected so I kept a special eye on him.

When Brenda went to fetch the car the girl started moaning so loudly I had to have a quiet word in her ear again, explaining that if she didn't keep quiet I'd have to ask my friend to deal with her again. After that she went as quiet as a mouse.

Two minutes later Brenda had parked the car outside the back door and was back in the house.

The boyfriend went into the car first, in the boot, then it was the girl's turn. We put her in the back seat, buckling her in so that she would be nice and safe. After that we switched out the house lights, made sure the gas was off, locked the door and left. The whole episode had taken less than fifteen minutes.

The drive to the farmhouse took us nearly forty-five minutes because we were driving extra carefully and well within the speed limit all the time. We didn't get so much as a peep out of the girl during the entire journey.

When we pulled up at the farm, Brenda started to giggle again. "We're home, Sarah," she said, just like she was speaking to a pal. That's when I gave her another sharp look because I thought she was talking too much, but she just grinned back at me. I thought there was a wild look in her eyes and that set the alarm bells ringing for me. I was going to speak to her about it, but by the time we got them into the farmhouse, she seemed to have calmed down again.

We'd planned to keep Our Sarah in the cellar, which was safe and secure, but now that we had had two guests we had to go to Plan B as I called it: the boyfriend went down into the cellar, where we could keep him under lock and key and Our Sarah was put in the bedroom. We were going to sleep on a sleeper couch in the living room.

We handcuffed her hand and foot to the heavy old brass bed in the room and we closed the curtains so that if anyone did happen to walk by, they weren't going to see anything. We chained the boyfriend to an iron ring that was fixed to one wall down in the cellar. The chain was long enough to give him some freedom of movement, but not long enough for him to get off the bed or reach the door or the window.

When they were safely tied up we took the gags off, but left the blindfolds on. After that, we took them both a cup of tea, Sarah first.

"We just want you to feel welcome," I said.

By this time she seemed to have calmed down, got herself under control, I mean.

"Is it money you want? My father will give you all the money you need. All you have to do is just let us both go."

That was when Brenda made her flinch by patting her on the cheek.

"We know that, Sarah, dear," she whispered, "We know that."

The boyfriend didn't say a thing when we took his tray down. He just sat cross-legged on the bed, still as a statue with his face turned away.

I put the car in the barn then returned to the house. In the living room we hugged each other. It was nearly midnight but we were still pumped up with adrenalin.

"So far, so good," I said.

We were both grinning because Part 1 of the operation had gone off without a hitch, apart from having an extra guest, that is.

Brenda put her hands on my shoulders and kissed me on the mouth. "They never knew what hit them," she whispered.

She was pleased with herself, anyone could see that, but I thought she'd been reckless, talking like she did.

"We need to stick to the plan," I said, "and we don't lay a hand – or foot – on them unless it's absolutely necessary, okay?"

She laughed when I said that, about the foot, I mean.

"You're just soft."

"No, I'm not soft," I said, "I'm just being cautious. Sooner or later we might need their co-operation about something. A willing partner is better than one who's been coerced."

"If they're shit scared they'll do whatever we tell them."

"Yes, but if the girl goes hysterical, we'll have big problems."

That was when she gave me a withering look. "Just what are you trying to say, Matthew?" she said.

"I'm trying to say that you're acting irresponsibly. By talking too much."

"It doesn't make any difference."

"Of course it makes a difference! The more you speak, the more likely it is they'll recognise you."

"So?"

"Not talking is part of the plan – remember?"

That was when she shrugged, like it didn't matter. I knew what was coming.

"You're just over-reacting."

"No, I'm not over-reacting! We have to stick to the plan."

She needed to think about that for a moment. "Fuck the plan," she said finally.

I was absolutely furious then and it was difficult for me to keep my voice down.

"Do you want to be caught?" I said. "Do you want to go to prison for the rest of your life?"

I expected her to argue, to start ranting and raving even, but instead she went very quiet. "Well, do you?" I asked, when she didn't answer.

She closed her eyes again, thought about it some more. "No," she said eventually.

"Then we need to be careful. Both of us."

"Yes, I know. I'm sorry. I stepped out of line. It won't happen again."

To be honest, the fact that she apologised so suddenly caught me on the wrong foot. Sometimes her moods changed so quickly I couldn't keep up.

"You have to remember that something can easily go wrong," I said, making an effort to sound reasonable.

"Yes, you're right," she said. "It's my fault, I'm sorry."

I didn't know whether to keep on at her, or let the matter drop. In the end, I let the matter drop.

"Let's just make sure it doesn't happen again, okay?"

She dropped her eyes and nodded. "Okay," she said.

Maybe if I'd really put my foot down then and been harder on her, we might have avoided the catastrophe that happened later on, but I just thought she was jumpy. And I thought that if I pushed too hard it would only make matters worse.

After that we talked about the boyfriend. Brenda wanted to know what we were going to do about him.

"We're going to use him as a bargaining tool," I said. "But first we need to find out more about him. His name, where he works, everything we…"

"It's Bowers," Brenda said, interrupting me.

"What?"

"His name – it's Bowers. Rod Bowers."

She'd never mentioned his name before.

"How do you know?"

She shrugged like it wasn't anything important. "It was in one of the newspaper articles."

I gave her a long hard look. I had the feeling there was something she wasn't telling me.

"What else do you know about him?" I asked.

"Nothing."

"Nothing?"

"Nothing."

There was something about the way she answered that made me think she was lying.

FIFTEEN

WE HAD ORIGINALLY PLANNED to contact the girl's parents the next day, but since everything had gone so smoothly, we decided to move things along a little. It was a change of plan, I said, but one that was justified by circumstances. Also, neither of us could sleep, we were much too hyped up for that.

At one o'clock I got the car out of the barn again and drove the twenty miles to the next town where I made the phone call. The phone rang at least twenty times before it was picked up.

"Who is this?" a woman said. She was very angry, I could tell that straight away, but she still sounded very la-di-da, like she'd got a plum in her mouth.

I had a handkerchief over the mouthpiece to disguise my voice.

"Is that Mrs Fitzgibbon?" I asked.

"Do you not know what time it is?" she said.

That's when I told her to keep her mouth shut and listen. That made her hesitate, but not for long, "To whom do you think you're speaking?" she said.

I suddenly had this ridiculous picture of her standing by the telephone dressed in ermine and pearls.

"You'll do what you're told," I said very calmly, "if you ever want to see your daughter alive again, that is."

The phone went silent. I could almost hear her thinking.

"Who is this?" she asked, but more cautiously this time. Then, when I didn't answer. "Is Sarah alright?"

I needed to keep the initiative. "She's alright – for the moment," I said.

"I want to know who's speaking," she said, trying to sound authoritative.

"Jack the Ripper."

I think she was beginning to think the whole thing was some kind of practical joke. "I shall call the police," she said, as if that was supposed to frighten me.

"Call the police and you'll never see your daughter alive again," I said.

This time there was a longer pause. "I don't know what you're talking about."

"I'm talking about your daughter, about Sarah. I have her. If you ever want to see her alive, you'd better get ready to pay."

"I don't know..." she began, but I'd already put down the phone.

When I got back to the house, Brenda was waiting for me, excited. "Well?" she said.

"I spoke to her mother. I think I got her out of bed."

We were whispering, trying not to let our guests hear.

"What about her father? Didn't you speak to him?"

"No, but I'm sure Mrs Fitzgibbon will pass on the message."

I'd put on a posh voice, pretending to be Mrs F and we both grinned.

"How have our two lovebirds been acting?" I asked.

"He's been as quiet as a mouse, but she's a pain in the arse."

As if on cue, Sarah called out, "Let me go. Please let me go," her voice echoing through the house.

"We need to shut her up," Brenda said.

"Yes, I know."

She picked up the roll of masking tape, which was lying on the kitchen table, and headed for the bedroom. When I didn't immediately follow, she gave me a look. "You may have to help me, Matthew," she said sharply.

The girl tried to push herself up against the back wall when she heard us come in.

Brenda went straight over to the bed. "You just don't learn, do you, Sarah?" she said equably.

The girl was whimpering, almost wetting herself with fear. "Please..." she said.

"Now, Sarah," she began very business-like, "because you don't seem to be able to keep quiet, we have to put your gag back on."

When the girl started to protest, Brenda shushed her, and then waited patiently until she had her full attention again.

"As I was saying, we have to put your gag back on. Now, when I take the pillowcase off your head, you will keep your eyes firmly shut, is that clear?"

"Is that clear, Sarah?" Brenda repeated, when she didn't answer.

There was a whispered, "Yes".

"Good."

The girl was shivering, out of control really, but she kept her eyes closed and in the end there was no struggle, just complete capitulation.

"A fucking lot of good you were," Brenda said, when we were back in the living room.

She was Dr Jekkyl and Mr Hyde: cool and calm one minute, angry and violent the next.

"You seemed to manage alright without me," I said.

Instead of answering, she went to sit at the kitchen table with her back to me, sulking, but I just let her stew.

Before going to bed I did a last check on our two guests. He had been lying on the bed, but sat up when he heard the door open.

"We'll pay you," he said quietly as I was turning to leave. "We'll pay you to let us go without harm."

Brenda started tugging at my arm even before I had a chance to respond.

"We don't speak to them," she whispered. "Remember, what you said, we don't speak to them," which was ironic I thought, coming from her.

The girl was crying, of course, her head buried in the pillow. Brenda stood watching her for a moment from the doorway then pulled the door closed. She was shaking her head and smiling when I got into bed with her. "Pathetic," she said. "Absolutely pathetic," and I knew she was talking about the girl.

We were both ready for sex that first night, Brenda especially. I think it was because we were so hyped up. What also made it exciting was trying to keep quiet, knowing that both of them were probably listening to us.

I think it was the best sex I've ever had, which is saying something considering what Brenda is like. I think Brenda felt the same as me, so at the end we were both hot and sweaty and breathing hard.

Afterwards we dozed off, but neither of us slept properly, not under the circumstances. For one thing, the sleeper couch wasn't as comfortable as a real bed and for another we were both too keyed up by the kidnapping.

At about four o'clock in the morning Brenda got up and made us both a cup of tea, which we drank in bed, whispering to each other in the dark.

"What do you think her mother will have done?" she said.

"The first thing I'd have done was to try to phone Our Sarah and her boyfriend," I said, "to see if the call was a hoax or not, then I'd probably have gone round to her house."

"She likes to burn the candle at both ends, does our Sarah. Maybe her mum thought she'd gone to an all-night rave or something like that?"

It was only much later, when the story came out, that we learned she'd phoned the police the second I'd put down the phone. Not that they did anything, not until the next morning that is. There was some fuss about that later on, the fact that the police didn't react as quickly as they should have done, I mean, but I gather that as far as they were concerned, it was hardly a police matter when a young woman who has a reputation for wild behaviour stays out all night.

The plan was to phone Our Sarah's parents again about 11 o'clock the next day. That was to give them time to think things over, but we didn't want to leave it too late because we wanted to keep them off balance, to maintain the initiative, so to speak.

After the tea we both lay awake in the darkness, not speaking a great deal, waiting for the dawn. I couldn't help being nervous, which is why I kept getting up to go to check on them. Once I heard a car go past in the lane and for a split second I thought it was the police coming to arrest us. I jumped out of bed so fast I almost had a heart attack.

Brenda looked at me like I'd gone mad, of course. "Just calm down, okay?" she said, "just calm down."

I made a show of wiping my brow, trying to make a joke of it, but I couldn't stop my hands shaking for twenty minutes after that.

SIXTEEN

AT SEVEN O'CLOCK the next morning we took our guests some tea and toast for breakfast. We made them keep the blindfolds on but loosened their hands, just enough so they could feed themselves. We were always very cautious but I couldn't help feeling that sooner or later they'd find a way to get free and get the jump on us. When I said this to Brenda she said I was being stupid.

Of course, when I took the tape off Our Sarah's mouth she started pleading with me again, begging me to let her go and that kind of thing, but I didn't say a word. Her boyfriend in the cellar maintained the same stoical silence all the time.

"We need to keep a special eye on him," I said to Brenda when we were back in the kitchen.

"He'll do as he's told, will our Rod," she said, like there was absolutely nothing to worry about.

When we went back to collect the cups and plates fifteen minutes later, neither of them had touched the food, which wasn't so surprising under the circumstances, I suppose. True to character, Our Sarah started begging and pleading again the moment we entered the room.

When we ignored her, she started sobbing uncontrollably and that was when Brenda couldn't contain herself. She stood by the door, waiting for Our Sarah to stop crying, then went over to the bed.

I was holding my breath, half expecting more violence.

"You make me sick," she whispered. "You make me sick you're so pathetic."

I'd never heard so much hatred in a voice before.

The girl started shivering with terror. Then she began sobbing again so Brenda put the tape back over her mouth.

"Fucking pathetic!" she said, when she walked out of the room,

"Completely fucking pathetic."

The boyfriend started to talk to us when we went to collect his breakfast things. "If you let us go now you won't be in such big trouble," he said.

Neither of us answered, which seemed to encourage him to carry on.

"If you call the whole thing off, we can say it was a kind of unfortunate mistake. Just walk away now and no one will come looking for you. Just let us go, unharmed. That way there won't be any real damage done."

I was amazed how fair and reasonable he sounded, like he was doing us a favour or something, but underneath his words there was still a suggestion of warning, a threat of dire consequences, if we didn't do what he wanted. We didn't answer him.

"What did I tell you about him?" I said to Brenda when we were out in the kitchen again.

"Cocky bastard, isn't he?" she said, but I could tell she was impressed. Most men under the circumstances would have been quivering in their boots, but he was making veiled threats.

"Like I said, we need to keep a special eye on him."

"You just leave him to me," Brenda said, almost like she was looking forward to the job.

At 11 o'clock I went out to telephone the parents again. The phone was picked up on the first ring, this time by her father.

"Is that Mr Fitzgibbon?" I asked.

Instead of answering, he just got straight down to business.

"Is my daughter safe?" he asked.

"Yes, for the time being."

"And Rod?"

"We had to invite him along as our guest."

I could hear him breathing. I guessed his wife was in the room with him, listening. I wondered if anyone else was listening too.

"What do you want?"

There was a hint of challenge in his voice. He wasn't the kind of man who was used to being pushed around.

"Money," I said. "Half a million pounds, in nice small bills."

That made him laugh. "And where do you think I'm going to get that from?" he asked.

"The bank. Where else?"

"No, I can't do it."

It was a flat statement of fact. He wasn't one to plead. He just gave the facts. But I'd done my homework. He had assets worth twice that much.

"I'm not a fool," I snapped back.

In the background I heard his wife say, "Please, Henry…" before he shushed her.

"Look, what you read about and what we have are two different things. This house is heavily mortgaged as are the other properties I own. Even if I have the money on paper, that's not the same as having it in cash."

I had no intention of carrying on a conversation about this.

"Then I suggest you have a conversation with your bank manager," I said. "This is not a subject that's open for debate." Then I put down the phone.

I went and had a cup of coffee then phoned back an hour later from a different telephone. Again, he answered on the first ring.

"Are you ready to discuss the details now?" I asked.

"I need to know that my daughter's safe."

"She's safe," I said.

"I want proof. Sarah is a very headstrong young woman. For all I know she may just have gone away without telling us, and you're taking advantage. She's done it before, gone away, I mean."

I laughed at this.

"I need to know for sure," he said.

"You get the money, I'll get proof," I said.

He started to say something but I put down the phone. I'd seen too many films about the police tracing phone calls to hang about too long. And I also wanted to keep him on his toes and off balance.

When I got back to the house I could see that Brenda was seething with anger. When I asked her what the problem was she said that the girl was getting stroppy.

"What does that mean?" I asked.

"I've just taken her some soup. She complained about the food. Said that she didn't want to eat the shit we were giving her. What does she think this is, a five star hotel?"

I went to see the girl. The soup was on side table, untouched. We'd decided on soup, which they could eat through a straw, because that way we wouldn't have to untie their hands or take their blindfolds off.

Our Sarah was sitting up in bed and her dress had ridden up high on her thighs and she looked very sexy. I couldn't help thinking that. Brenda caught me looking at her in a particular way and for a moment I thought she was going to say something, but she didn't. In the end she just walked away and left the two of us together.

"I hear you're unhappy with the food," I said.

"I don't like mushroom soup," she said.

"Then you'll go hungry."

When I turned to leave she said, "What are you going to do with us?"

"We're going to keep you here until your daddy pays us some money."

"So you're blackmailing him?"

"I don't like that word," I said. "I prefer to think of it as returning something of value and being rewarded for my efforts."

She smiled at that, then changed her position on the bed, exposing a bit more leg for me to admire. That was when I realised that it was all a ploy to ensnare me. She was a very attractive young woman and I'm sure this kind of thing had always worked for her in the past.

"My father is not as rich as you think he is," she said. "His businesses have not been going so well lately. He's had some labour problems and his competitors have been giving him a hard time."

"Yes, but I'm sure that you have been a great comfort to him," I replied, cynical like.

She shrugged, like it was a matter of little concern. "I wasn't always the best of daughters," she admitted.

"Your father's a rich man," I said.

"Yes, he's a rich man. But he's not as rich as he was five years ago. And now there's a strike going on. How much are you asking?"

I thought that getting into a conversation with her was the worst thing I could do because that was making me see her as a "person" rather than as an "object", but I was interested to see what her reaction would be, even though I could guess what it was even before she spoke.

"Half a million pounds," I answered.

She shook her head. "He hasn't got that kind of money."

"Then he'll have to get it, won't he?"

That was when Brenda walked in. I could tell from the look on her face that she wasn't happy. "I think you've talked enough," she said.

The girl moved and made an attempt to pull down her dress. Brenda is jealous, I thought.

"He can't get that much money, don't you understand?" she called out as I was leaving the room.

Of course, Brenda was annoyed that we'd had such a long conversation.

"We weren't going to talk to them," she said. "That was your rule, not mine."

I said that I needed to get her reaction to the ransom.

"But we both know what she'll say. She'll say her father can't afford it."

I knew she was right, but I didn't want to debate the issue.

"Maybe," I said.

"So what are we going to do about the boyfriend?" she asked, changing the subject.

He was a problem that neither of us had expected.

"We keep him here until the ransom's paid," I said.

She shook her head. "I think he's going to cause us a lot of trouble. I know his sort."

When I smiled at the remark, Brenda became angry again.

"Don't patronise me," she said. "He's a liar. A cheat. Devious is what he is."

"How do you know?" I asked.

That's when she gave me a look I'd never seen before. I think she was about to say something, but then she stopped herself. I suddenly got the uncomfortable feeling she knew a lot more about the boyfriend than she'd been letting on. That's when it dawned on me.

"You know him, don't you?" I said.

That seemed to make her even more furious, if that was possible. "Don't be an idiot!" she shouted, then when she saw I still didn't believe her, "No, I don't know him. But he's a troublemaker. I know his sort."

I was going to ask her some more questions, but she walked away and out into the yard, before I had the chance.

I followed her out of the house. It was a chill afternoon: damp ground under a grey sky.

"There's something you're not telling me," I said.

"No, there's not!" Then when she could see I wasn't convinced. "Look, he's a clever, conniving bastard, anyone can see that. We have to be careful of him."

"He hasn't seen our faces, he doesn't know who we are."

We were standing at the end of the house. Normally Brenda was confident, had all the answers, but now she looked and sounded nervous, uncertain.

A small brown bird flew out of the barn and swooped down towards the river.

"Imagine what he might have picked up when the police question him," she said. "All the little facts and figures. Who knows what they'll be able to work out."

"So what are you saying we do with him?"

She turned to stare at me, lowered her voice, like she thought someone might be listening.

"I think we have to kill him," she whispered.

I would have laughed if she hadn't been so serious.

"You're mad," I said.

"No, I'm not mad. I'm just trying to protect us. "

"I don't see how killing him is going to protect us."

"It will if he can lead the police to us."

When I didn't answer, she carried on. "I remember you telling me that some people have the right to impose their will on others."

"Impose their will," I said, "not kill them."

She shrugged. "I don't see the difference."

"Don't be so stupid," I said. I couldn't help myself.

That's when she started to flare up again.

"It's not stupid, it's logical."

"Killing someone isn't logical. And it isn't part of the plan."

I couldn't believe I was having this conversation.

"Plans change. Kidnapping the boyfriend wasn't part of the plan either!"

"If we kill him and not her it will make things worse for us."

"No, it won't. It will just halve our chances of getting caught."

She seemed so matter-of-fact, like the whole thing was already decided. I knew I had to put my foot down.

"I'm not going to kill him," I said.

"No one's asking you to."

"What does that mean?"

"It means no one's asking you to," she repeated, but this time her eyes were blazing.

She was talking murder and I was horrified. At first I thought she'd come unhinged, but then I realised she was actually quite calm about the whole thing, that it was me who was agitated, not her.

"You're mad," I said again, "stark raving mad." Then I walked away and went back into the house. It was either that or have a flaming row, which wouldn't have done either of us any good. What angered me most was the way Brenda had made a decision without consulting me. She was becoming more and more unpredictable by the day, which was a worrying development.

To give myself something to do I went down to the cellar to see how Rod was doing. He was lying on the bed when I went in and I thought he was sleeping, but he sat up the moment I opened the door. He tried to start up a conversation again, but I told him to shut up, in no uncertain terms.

I made him turn over so I could check his chains, all the time thinking about what Brenda had said.

When I turned to go back up into the main house she was standing at the top of the steps, watching us. The cold look she'd had in her eyes when I'd walked back into the cottage had gone. Suddenly, she was just Brenda the secretary again.

"He's a dangerous one, that one," she whispered to me when I closed the door on the cellar.

I walked past her shaking my head. I was still angry with her. "I don't know what you mean," I said.

"I mean – he's going to cause us a lot of trouble one way or another."

"You're becoming paranoid," I said.

"No, I'm not becoming paranoid, I'm just looking after our best interests," she answered.

SEVENTEEN

AT TEN O'CLOCK the next morning – the Sunday – I phoned the Fitzgibbons again.

I'd assumed from the start that the police would be monitoring all the phone calls so I always telephoned from a different call box, usually from a different town, too.

The moment her father answered the phone I could tell straight away that his attitude was different, more compliant this time.

"Have you got the money?" I asked.

"I can't get that much money together at such short notice."

I would have been surprised if he'd said anything else, but I wasn't going to take any shit from him. "I don't think you're taking me seriously," I said.

"I am. I mean it, I am. But you've got to realise that it's not that easy to get hold of such a lot of money at short notice."

"Do you remember John Paul Getty Junior?" I asked.

There was a pause. I'd caught him on the wrong foot.

"His kidnappers cut off his ear," I said. "Is that what you want me to do? Send you one of your daughter's ears?"

The panic came into his voice straight away. "No, don't hurt her. Please."

"Then don't piss me about!"

"Please be reasonable. I need time. It's the weekend. And I have to know that my daughter's safe."

"She's safe... for now."

"Yes, but I don't know that. I must know for sure that she's safe."

"If you know your daughter's safe, we get the money. Yes?"

"Yes. You'll get the money... I promise."

He sounded sincere, genuine, but I wasn't going to let up just because I felt sorry for him. That was one emotion I couldn't afford.

"When?"

"I don't... I'm not... "

"WHEN?"

"Tomorrow," he said. "Tomorrow. Monday." I could hear the fear in his voice again.

"Like I said before, you get the money, I'll get the proof," I said and slammed down the phone.

When I got back to the farmhouse at lunchtime I went to check on our two guests again.

Before I went down into the cellar, I stood at the top of the steps for a long time. Rod knew I was there, of course. I could tell that because even though he was blindfolded, he kept his face towards me all the time, though he didn't say anything. All he did was sit quietly, which was a lot more unnerving for some reason than if he'd been thrashing about or cursing and swearing. I'm becoming as paranoid as Brenda, I thought.

To make myself feel easier, I had him hold up his arms so that I could see he was still locked up, but I still felt nervous. The more I thought about it, the more I knew that Brenda was right: we were bound to be giving away subtle clues about ourselves all the time, but that still didn't mean I wanted to kill him.

Up in the kitchen Brenda was doing the washing up.

"There's no reason for violence," I said to her.

She carried on what she was doing, didn't turn to look at me even. "You mean you think we're just going to take the money, set them free then go back to life as normal?"

"Yes. Why not?"

She shook her head then pulled the plug out of the sink. While the water was gurgling away, she dried her hands on a towel. Then she turned to me.

"Because, Matthew, if we do that, even if we get away with it, we'll be looking over our shoulders for the rest of our lives."

"They don't know anything about us," I said.

"Of course they do! They know you're a man, they know I'm a woman. They know we have a farm or some kind of hideaway in the country."

She smiled when I reminded her that they were blindfolded when we brought them in, that they'd never seen the inside of the house.

"You can tell this is a farmhouse or somewhere out of the city just from the feel of the place. Your ears will tell you that."

"Not necessarily," I said, but I knew I didn't sound convincing.

"We're in too deep to pull out now."

"No one's talking about pulling out."

"We've got to be realistic. We're going to have trouble with him."

"No, we're not. Everything's going perfectly to plan."

For a long moment she stared at me, then she said very condescendingly, "Oh, I'm sorry, Matthew, I didn't realise."

She was like a stuck record: he was going to be a problem and sooner or later we were going to have to deal with him.

"We won't have any problems if we're careful," I said.

That made her laugh. "Let's not deceive ourselves, shall we?"

It suddenly occurred to me that that she was becoming as big a problem as he was, but I pushed that thought to the back of my mind.

"So what are you saying?" I asked.

"I'm saying we have to sort this out quickly. The longer we let things go on, the more problems we're going to have."

"You mean, from the boyfriend?"

"Yes, from him. And from her, too."

"Our job is to keep them here, then after we get the money we let them go," I said.

"And if they can recognise us, then what?"

"They can't recognise us. We've been careful."

"You're just saying that to protect her," she grinned. "That's because you fancy her!"

I knew something had been bothering her, now I knew what it was. She was jealous.

"I don't fancy her," I hissed. "This is business. Business! You don't have any reason to be jealous."

"Jealous?" she said, getting angry again, "I'm not jealous, I'm just thinking with my head not my dick." That was when she dropped her bombshell. "We have to kill them both."

"Are you completely insane?" I said.

"We're too far in to back out now," she said nastily.

I went to walk away, but she grabbed me by the arm, spinning me around. "You've got a better idea then, have you?" she asked all scathing like. "You got us into this shit and now you're going to get us out again?"

"Yes, I've got a better idea. We stick to our plan. We get the money. We let them go."

"We can't do that. They know too much."

"Then why didn't you say something when we were planning the whole thing?"

"Because I just did what you told me. That was one of your conditions, remember?"

So now it was my fault.

"And who's going to kill them," I asked, calling her bluff. "You?"

She shrugged, like it was no big deal. "Yes, if I have to," she said.

What scared me the most was that I could see that she meant it. That's when it struck me that Brenda wasn't just becoming a problem, she was becoming a liability – and sooner or later I was going to have to deal with her.

"Give it a rest, Brenda," I said. "Just give it a rest, okay?"

EIGHTEEN

THAT AFTERNOON I TAPE-RECORDED Our Sarah begging her father to pay us the money. I got her to make a reference to an item on the midday news so that he knew she was alive. I also got her to write a letter telling him to hand over the money without any trouble.

Just after dark, I drove into town and played the tape over the phone to him. This time I wasn't looking to get into a conversation.

"We want the money tomorrow," I said. "No more delays. Tomorrow."

He started to make excuses, but I cut him short. "Don't you fucking well understand?" I shouted. There was a muted yes, then I said: "Lunchtime tomorrow," and put down the phone.

After that I went back to the car and read the newspaper for an hour, then called again but from a different place.

"Tomorrow!" I screamed, when he answered. "Okay? No excuses – tomorrow!"

I slammed down the phone before he had chance to say anything.

I'd assumed from the beginning that he'd contact the police; that his living room would be filled with detectives listening on their headsets, like in the films. When I was walking back to my car I imagined them all pondering the call.

"He sounded nervous to me," one of them would say.

"Hysterical, more like," another would add.

"Yeah, desperate even."

I wanted them to think that. I wanted them to think I was unhinged, out of control even because that way, if they thought I was dangerous, they'd be more anxious to hand over the cash without giving me the run-around.

When I got back to the house, Brenda was waiting for me at the front door and there was a wild look in her eyes. When I walked into the cottage, she said, "He's dead."

I looked at her. For a moment the words didn't register.

"I've killed him."

The strange thing was, I wasn't even surprised. I felt numb; almost like I'd known all along that something like this was going to happen.

I didn't say anything. I just went down to the cellar and stood at the bottom of the stairs.

Still chained up, he was lying face down on the floor next to the bed. There was a dark pool of blood around his head and the murder weapon – a claw hammer I'd seen in the barn, blood-splattered at one end – was next to the body.

Suddenly, I couldn't breathe properly. Behind me, Brenda was babbling on like a lunatic, yet I still felt detached from it all, like it was a bad dream, that at any moment I'd wake up to find it was all a terrible mistake.

"He attacked me," I heard Brenda say. "I made him tea and he lunged at me when I went to put it down. I had to defend myself."

I knew she was lying, but I was too exhausted to say anything. When I slumped down on the steps she said, "We needed to get rid of him, Matthew. Sooner or later he would have caused us problems. I told you that."

She made it all sound so reasonable. She'd just killed a man, but she didn't care. I had a sudden urge to pick up the hammer and beat her senseless with it, but the moment passed.

"Does the girl know?"

"No."

"Are you sure?"

"There wasn't a struggle. He didn't make any noise," she said.

I could hear myself breathing. The whole thing was a nightmare. I had gone out to make a phone call and now there was a dead body in the house. I stood up and went to check the corpse: maybe she'd made a mistake? Maybe he was still alive? That, of course, was a forlorn hope.

"It will be better this way," she said when I was leaning over him. "Now he's out of the way, I mean. I said that he was a problem."

When I looked up at her, she was smiling. "This isn't a game, you fucking idiot," I said.

I saw her face change, saw the hatred, the absolute determination come into her eyes.

"Nobody said it was a game!"

I heard the contempt in her voice. I wanted to grab her by the shoulders, shake some sense into her, but I it was too late for all that.

"I don't know why you're so upset," she said scornfully. "Kidnapping or murder – what's the difference?"

"With murder you end up with a dead body in the cellar," I whispered.

I barged past her, went upstairs and sat at the kitchen table. A moment later she came and sat down opposite.

"We'll sort everything out, Matthew," she said gently, like that suddenly made everything alright.

"Don't you realise what you've done?" I said. Then, when she didn't answer: "Are you sure Sarah doesn't know?"

"No, she doesn't know."

That was when it struck me that Brenda had been planning to do this all along. All she'd been waiting for was the right opportunity.

"We have to get rid of the body," I said.

"We'll bury him tonight when she's asleep. Next to the house somewhere. Down by the riverbank."

"You've worked everything out, haven't you?" I said, but she didn't answer.

At one o'clock in the morning we went down into the cellar to bring up the body. At first, I took hold of his head and shoulders and Brenda got hold of his feet and we tried to carry him out that way, but he was too heavy and already starting to stiffen so the best we could do was stagger along for two or three paces before putting him down again. We knew we'd never get him up the stairs without making a racket and alerting Our Sarah, so I suggested we try to hoist him onto my shoulders fireman style and I'd drag him out that way.

That was easier said than done, believe me. First we had to prop him against a wall, which had us both panting, then I had to get in front of him and let him fall forwards so he was half lying on my back. In the end, that's how I got him up from the cellar, over my shoulders with his arms around my neck and his feet dragging up the steps.

When we opened the front door Our Sarah called out to us.

"Who's there?" she cried. "What are you doing?"

Brenda went and put her head in the bedroom.

"Shut the fuck up!" she said and we didn't hear a peep out of her after that.

We'd decided to bury his body on the riverbank beneath some bushes.

Working without a light, it took us over an hour to dig a hole big enough. Before we shoved him in, Brenda went through his pockets. He had about twenty pounds on him, which was the only thing we took. The credit cards and wallet he had in his back pocket, we didn't touch. After that, we shovelled the soil back into the grave then stamped it down as best we could. The last thing we did was spread some leaves and twigs around to make the site less conspicuous.

I was worried that some small animals might dig the body up, which is what I'd read sometimes happened.

When we went back into the house, Our Sarah was wide awake.

"Where have you been? What have you been doing?" she called out, but neither of us answered.

NINETEEN

I HARDLY SLEPT A WINK that night and I was out on the riverbank again at first light to see if the grave had been tampered with. It hadn't, although it was obvious from the way the surface of the ground had been disturbed that someone had done some digging.

An hour later we took Our Sarah some breakfast, but she didn't ask about her boyfriend. In fact, she didn't say anything, which was surprising considering she'd been such a talkative one up until then. It made me think she knew something bad had happened, which was a worrying development. It didn't bode well for the future.

I have to admit that it had occurred to me that Brenda could be right, that we could hardly let Our Sarah go free after we'd killed her boyfriend, but I tried not to think about that. I made a conscious effort to put such unpleasant thoughts to the back of my mind, kept telling myself that there had to be another way, that killing one person was a dreadful mistake, but killing two would be a complete disaster.

We had planned that I would go to work and Brenda would phone in sick so that she could look after the girl.

That Monday was probably the longest working day of my life. It was hard to concentrate, what with so many other things to worry about and I don't know how I got through it, but I did. At lunchtime I left work and telephoned Our Sarah's father again to make sure he'd got everything ready for the handover that night.

This time he was in a much more sober frame of mind.

"Have you got the money?" I asked.

"Yes. All I want is my daughter back."

"Then all you have to do is follow instructions. You do as you're told and there won't be any trouble," I said.

"What about Rod, Sarah's boyfriend?"

I suddenly felt panicked and my mouth went dry.

"I don't know what you're talking about," I said, which was a fool-ish thing to say, but he'd caught me on the wrong foot.

"Yes, you do! Her boyfriend, Rod. He was with her at the house. We spoke about him before. You kidnapped him as well, didn't you?"

"Who says we were at the house?" I said.

There was a pause. I could almost hear him thinking.

"Rod always stays at Sarah's on Friday nights. And there was a meal on the stove and the kitchen table was laid out for two."

It was so obvious I could have kicked myself, but you don't wash the dishes and put the crockery away when you're in the middle of a kid-napping a person.

"First things first," I said, meaning we have other things to talk about, but he wouldn't let the matter drop.

"You'll get your money, but what about Rod?"

"First things first," I repeated, angry this time.

He started to protest again, wanting to know what we'd done with him, but I cut him short. In the end he would only shut up when I threatened to put down the phone.

"I'm only here to talk about the money," I said, almost shouting. "Nothing else. I don't want to talk about any boyfriend. Understand?"

My hands were trembling and I knew I sounded like I was hiding something, but there was nothing else I could do under the circum-stances.

To calm myself down, I put my hand over the receiver and took three deep breaths before I spoke again.

"I want you to put the cash into a red holdall and to be ready to deliver it the next time I phone," I said, making an effort to keep my voice level.

"When will that be?"

"The next time I phone."

I heard him sigh. "Okay," he said, "just don't hurt my daughter."

"No one's going to get hurt as long as you do as you're told."

"Will my daughter be at the hand-over point?"

"We'll see."

I wanted to get off the phone, but the conversation wasn't going the way I'd intended.

"I need to know. I've promised you'll get your money. All I want is my daughter back safe and sound.

"Then all you have to do is exactly what I tell you."

"I want to know if she'll be at the place where I give you the money." He was getting authoritative again. Like I said, he wasn't used to taking orders for long.

"When I get the money, you'll get instructions where you can find her," I said.

He started to ask another question, but I'd already cut him off.

When I got back to work I went to see Mrs Williams to hand in my resignation. I'd decided I was going to go away after we'd got the money, abroad maybe.

"I'm giving you two weeks notice," I said.

I think she was angry, though she didn't say anything. She just put the letter in her in-tray and went back to the work she was doing. She didn't say a word. Not even, "Are you sure you won't reconsider, Matthew?" or "You'll be greatly missed, Matthew". Nothing. Five years of hard slog and that's all the thanks you get – nothing!

When I finally got back to the cottage after work I could see straightaway that Brenda was agitated.

The first thing she said to me when I walked through the door was, "We need to get rid of her."

I was really angry and shocked.

"We already have one murder on our hands, Brenda," I said. "We don't need another."

"She's just trouble," she said.

I was getting more and more anxious about Brenda. She was just too unpredictable. I thought she was completely mad, either that or she was just plain wicked. How else could you explain the way she was acting? Either way, I was worried.

" Why's that?" I asked, trying to stay patient.

"Because she can identify us."

"We don't know that. She's never seen our faces. If we hand her over and get the money, then I still think we can get away with the whole thing."

"Don't be so naïve!" It was like she was speaking to a small child.

I hated her then. She was just like Mrs Williams: she didn't care about anyone but herself. Murder had never been part of my plan, but that wasn't true for Brenda.

"You've been planning this all along, haven't you?" I asked.

"Don't be ridiculous," she answered, but I knew from the way she couldn't look me in the eyes that she was lying.

It felt like everything was unravelling, getting out of control, which is why I knew I had to put my foot down, to stop the rot so to speak.

"From now on you don't do anything without my say-so," I said.

I was expecting all sorts of argument, but all she did was shrug. "Okay," she said. Then she went and put the kettle on the stove. "I'm making her vegetable soup for supper," she said.

At six o'clock I went out and phoned Our Sarah's father and gave him instructions. He had a mobile phone so I told him to go to the post office in the high street at nine o'clock and to wait for us there with the money.

An hour later we took Our Sarah her supper. I had mixed some sleeping tablets in her soup because we wanted her out cold if we were going to leave her alone in the house.

She sat bolt upright in bed when we walked into the bedroom.

"Who's there?" she said.

"We've brought you something to eat," I said.

"How long are you going to keep me here?"

"We're going to meet your dad tonight," I said.

"To get the money?"

"Yes."

The truth was, we were intending to make that night a dry run, to make sure her father didn't have any unpleasant surprises up his sleeve, but I wasn't going to tell her that.

While we were talking, Brenda had put the tray down on the bed. She leaned over and I thought she was going to check the blindfold was properly in place, but the next thing I knew she had a kitchen knife in her hand. Our Sarah squealed when Brenda stabbed her in the neck. She kicked out, catching Brenda on the hip, shoving her backwards, but Brenda just grunted and went back onto the attack, plunging the knife into the girl's chest time after time. Twenty seconds later it was all over and the girl lay spread-eagled on her back, her dress up around her waist, her knickers showing. She was still twitching, but she was dead, anyone could see that.

There was blood and soup everywhere: all down the front of the girl, on the floor, on the walls, on the ceiling, dripping off Brenda. Everywhere.

She turned to me. "A lot of fucking good you were," she hissed.

She started wiping the knife on the sleeve of Our Sarah's dress: rapid, jerky movements to get it clean, first one side of the blade, then the other, over and over, until the steel was gleaming and there was blood running down her arm and onto the bed. At that moment Brenda didn't look human.

"What have you done?" I said.

I was shaking. I couldn't help it.

She started to unfasten the girl's handcuffs.

"I've saved your skin," she said. "That's what I've done!"

"You didn't have to do that!" I shouted. "You're mad, totally mad!" But she wasn't even listening. She was wrapping the girl in the bed sheets, dragging her off the bed and onto the floor.

"Jesus Christ, look at all the blood!"

"Pull yourself together," she said. Then, "We need to clean up before we go out. Get a bucket of water. A bucket of water and a towel." When I didn't move, she walked over and gave me a shove. "Now, Matthew," she said, "Now!"

Like a robot, I did what she told me. I got a bucket of water and a towel and began wiping the floor while Brenda knelt on the bed and worked at the walls. The dead girl wrapped up like a mummy was lying between us.

"We go ahead with the plan," she said, wiping down the skirting board. "Tonight we have a dry run, make the father run around for us. If we're happy, then we do the same tomorrow and take his money."

She had everything worked out. The dead girl was just an incon-venience. It felt like I was living a nightmare: I was in a state of shock, but for her everything was normal and matter-of-fact.

Brenda wasn't an asset anymore, she was a danger.

124

"You didn't have to kill her," I said, but she didn't even bother to answer.

Before we left the farm, we wrapped the girl's body in black plastic bags and dragged it over to the trees, making sure it was out of sight. Brenda would have left it where it was, but I knew I couldn't go back to that house knowing that there was a dead girl waiting for me in the bedroom.

After that we drove into town for our rendezvous with her father. About half a mile from the Post Office I dropped Brenda off and she strolled towards the meeting place while I went to find a public phone. At exactly nine o'clock I phoned him on his cell phone. He answered on the first ring.

"Go to the town square and pick up the phone outside the library when it rings," I said. "You have ten minutes."

Brenda and I had spent a lot of time working out exactly how the money was to be handed over. We were working on the assumption that the police would be trying to track the old man's every move, so we'd decided to carry out a dry run, just to make sure things worked out like we planned. And even though the whole thing was just for practice, we'd still worked out the route down to the last detail and timed every part of the journey so we could keep an eye on him from a safe distance. That way, if he tried to get up to any tricks we'd be able to spot it straight away.

For the next hour we had him moving from place to place, one of us watching him all the time, to make sure he wasn't getting up to any funny business. He ended up back at the phone box outside the library, which is where I'd put the letter his daughter had written, hidden in one of the telephone books. That was when I told him that the whole escapade had been a practice run to make sure he hadn't got the police involved.

"We'll do the same thing tomorrow night," I said. "Be ready to leave at a moment's notice."

"Will tomorrow be a practice run?" he asked.

He was panicked, I could tell that from his voice.

"You'll never know, will you?" I said. "We'll keep doing this until we're satisfied you're not setting us up."

"The police don't know anything about this. I just want my daughter back," he said.

We later found out he was telling the truth. They never pursued the daughter-gone-missing story with the local police after that first phone call because they were afraid things would go wrong.

"Tomorrow," I said. Then I put the phone down.

TWENTY

I COULD SMELL BLOOD WHEN I walked back into the cottage.

"We have to get rid of the stink," I said.

We stripped down to our underclothes to give the bedroom another going over, this time using bleach and scouring powder. I also said that I was going to come back the next weekend to repaint the entire room.

After that we went out to the riverbank again in our underclothes, even though it was raining. We dug another hole about a metre deep next to the boyfriend's grave and then rolled Our Sarah's body into it.

After we'd replaced all the soil Brenda stamped over the grave, packing the earth down before we pulled twigs and branches over the spot. By this time we were freezing cold and covered in mud and our shoes were ruined.

"It's romantic, isn't it?" she said. "Now the two lovers can be together for all eternity."

Even though her teeth were chattering she was grinning like it was all a big joke.

"Is that your idea of being funny?" I asked angrily.

She gave me a long look then started to giggle.

"You've no sense of humour, have you, Matthew?" she said.

By the time we got into bed after we'd showered, it was nearly two o'clock in the morning. We'd made up the sleeper couch in the lounge because that was the only room that didn't have any demons for me, but I couldn't fall asleep. I kept drifting off then waking up, kept seeing the girl's body dissolve into the ground as we shovelled the dirt over it. In the end, I just lay awake in the darkness, listening to the rain, wondering just how I was going to carry on like a normal person after what we'd done. Next to me, Brenda slept like a log.

Just before dawn, I went down to the river again to check on the graves. Even though we'd tried to camouflage the place, the whole area was churned up into a quagmire. I spread some more twigs and branches around, but I'm not sure it made all that much difference.

When I got back to the house Brenda was already up and about in the kitchen, waiting for me. I could tell by the way she was banging cups and saucers around in the sink that she was upset about something.

"What's wrong with you?" I demanded.

"I think you're getting cold feet," she said.

"What's that supposed to mean?"

"You're losing your nerve."

I could feel my hands shaking so I put them in my pockets.

"It's a bit late for you to be worried about that now," I snapped back.

"You're not happy about killing them, are you?"

I couldn't believe what I was hearing. Hadn't she heard anything I'd said?

"Of course I'm not happy! I told you that all along. Killing them wasn't in the plan. I didn't plan on murder."

"You didn't actually think that we'd be able to kidnap someone and keep them here for a few days and then let them go, did you?"

"Yes. Why not?"

The look she gave me was pure incredulity.

"Then you're even more dense that I thought you were."

"There was no reason to kill them," I said.

She closed her eyes for a moment. When she opened them again she gave me one of her dry little smiles.

"Of course there fucking was!"

I started to walk away. "I can't talk to you any more," I said.

That's when her whole demeanour changed. One second she was a screaming harpy and the next the voice of reason, but I knew it was just an act.

"Look, Matthew, I'm sorry," she said suddenly all apologetic, "but the truth is we'd never have gotten away with it. This way we can both go back to work and we don't have to worry about either of them escaping or leading the police to us. And after we've got the money, we can give up our jobs, go to live somewhere else... overseas, maybe."

"The truth is you think you've got everything all worked out, don't

128

you?" I said.

"I'm just thinking about our futures."

"You make me sick," I said. I couldn't help myself.

On the way back into town that morning, I told Brenda that I'd handed in my notice at Thompsons. I expected a lot of argument about me making decisions without asking her and that kind of thing, but all she said was, "Well, it's probably something you should have done a long time ago," and left it at that.

When I pulled up outside her flat she kissed me on the cheek before getting out of the car. She seemed happy to pretend that everything was completely normal, that we hadn't killed two people and buried their bodies on a riverbank.

"If we walk away now and cut our losses we might be able to get away with it," I said.

"But that's the reason we did the kidnapping – for the money."

"Yes, but now there are two dead bodies on our conscience."

"So?"

"So that puts a different complexion on things."

"Not for me it doesn't."

"It does for me," I said.

"Then that's something you're going to have to work on, isn't it, Matthew?" she answered.

When Brenda strolled into work at nine-thirty that morning she was all bright and breezy, laughing and joking with the other girls. At lunchtime she came into my office after everybody had gone off to the canteen, even though I'd told her we should keep out of each other's way for a few days.

I'd been thinking about getting the money all morning. That is, I'd been thinking about not getting the money.

"If we don't contact the parents again, we might get away with it," I said, after she'd sat down.

"Get away with what?"

"The murders."

I could tell from the look on her face that she didn't agree.

"We've had this discussion before, Matthew," she said, very sancti-monious-like. "We've earned the money and whether or not we get the ransom now won't make a scrap of difference to Ms Fitzgibbon and her boyfriend."

"I thought that the reason we did what we did was for the thrill of it," I said. "The money was a just a bonus."

"Not any more it isn't."

That's when I finally said what I'd been thinking all morning.

"You enjoyed killing them, didn't you, Brenda?" I said.

She gave me a long, searching look, a look I couldn't fathom. In the end, though, I think she just threw caution to the wind.

"Yes, of course," she answered. "Who wouldn't?"

She laughed when she saw the expression of horror on my face. "Don't you remember what you told me about the supermen?" she asked. "You said that superior people had the right to do as they please. Well, that's what we are – superior people. That means we have the right to do what we want to our victims."

"I don't think the police or her family will see it that way," I said.

"Fuck the police! And fuck the parents, too!" she said, grinning.

"You're a monster, a bloodthirsty monster," I said. I couldn't help myself, but I think she thought I was joking.

"Yes, and I'm going to be a fucking rich one after tonight," she said giggling out loud again.

I picked Brenda up outside her flat at seven o'clock then went to find a telephone, and while I was giving Sarah's old man his instructions, she was in the telephone box with me, whispering in my ear, urging me on, insistent.

"We're going to get the money, Matthew," she kept saying. "You hear me, we're going to get the money."

After that, Brenda put on her disguise in the back of the car while I was driving to the first meeting point.

Sarah's old man arrived right on time – carrying the same holdall he'd had with him the night before.

At the first contact point I sent him to a second, at the second contact point I sent him to a third and so on.

After he'd been running from place to place for nearly an hour, Brenda stationed herself on the route we knew he'd have to take to get to the next rendezvous. It was a busy street and when he came walking down the road, she stepped out of the shop doorway where she'd been waiting for him and said, "Give me the holdall". He didn't seem to realise what was happening until she said, "Give it to me now if you want to see Sarah alive!"

She tugged the bag out of his arms before he had chance to answer and started to walk away. That's when he turned to follow her, but she waved him away.

"Carry on to the next meeting point," she said.

"But what about my daughter?"

"Wait for a phone call," she shouted and moved off into the crowd.

She walked through a late-night shopping centre and made her way to the multi-storey car park at the back. I'd already stationed myself on one of the balconies from where I could watch her, to give her a signal if anyone was following. By the time I got back to my car, she had already changed back into her ordinary clothes and had the bag open on her knees, counting the money.

"Is it all there?" I asked.

"Oh, yes," she said, grinning, "it's all here."

Half an hour later we were both back at my flat. In the kitchen we counted the money properly just to confirm that it was all there. It was.

How long Sarah's father waited for a phone call, we never did find out. To be honest, I almost felt sorry for him, but that episode was over so I made a concerted effort to put any unpleasant thoughts to the back of my mind. What we have to do now is just get on with things, I told myself.

The next day we went back to work as normal. There was no mention of the kidnapping in the press or on the TV, which surprised me at the time, to be quite honest, but now I know that old man Fitzgibbon waited in hope for a couple of days for his daughter to get in touch with him, before he went to the police.

TWENTY-ONE

LIKE BEFORE, WE SPLIT the money 50/50. I kept half and Brenda kept half.

At the weekend I didn't want to go back to the farm like I'd intended because I couldn't stop thinking about the bodies down by the river. But I knew that if we were going to get away with it we'd have to act normal and make sure our tracks were well covered. That meant making sure the gravesite wasn't discovered and painting out the bedroom. Also, if we were around the farmhouse all the time there was less chance of any snoopers accidentally stumbling onto something they shouldn't.

That Friday, the Friday after the kidnapping, the story came out. It was in the local paper in the morning and on the national news at eight o'clock that night. On the TV, after a police officer had sketched out the details of the abduction, Sarah's father made an appeal for anyone with information to come forward.

The strange thing is, it was only when I saw him in the flesh so to speak that it actually became real for me. Up until then it had been a kind of dream, dismembered voices on the telephone, that kind of thing, which sounds ridiculous, I know, but now it was headline news and everyone was talking about it. There was even a lot of discussion at work, different people coming up with all sorts of weird and wonderful theories, none of them remotely near the truth, of course.

I could tell that Brenda was excited that the story was front-page news, but I was just worried. Paranoid, Brenda called it, but I couldn't help having a bad feeling about the whole thing. I kept reviewing all the steps we'd taken. I mean, I knew we'd been very careful, but there was no way of telling what someone had seen or heard that could throw a spanner in the works.

That Saturday we went back to the farm again. I'd liked the place at first. It was quiet and peaceful and quite beautiful in its own way, but now there were two dead bodies buried outside the cottage so that spoilt it for me.

Of course, the first thing I did when we got there was go down to the riverbank to check on the graves, which were undisturbed, thank goodness. The spot where Our Sarah and her boyfriend were buried was darker than the surrounding area, but there'd been quite a lot of rain that week and that seemed to have settled the ground so you'd hardly notice any difference unless you knew exactly where to look.

Brenda, of course, was her usual happy-go-lucky self. She was still excited about the whole thing, like she was a celebrity or something, and she'd bought every newspaper she could lay her hands on to read all the articles about the kidnapping.

One thing that interested me about the newspaper reports was that all of a sudden Our Sarah had become a "high-spirited, fun-loving" girl, whereas while she'd been alive it had been all the reporters could do to avoid calling her a drunken bitch.

I remember saying this to Brenda one time. It was just an innocuous comment, but she went completely overboard. "You did fancy her, didn't you?" she accused.

I never had, not really anyway. I mean she was good looking and she had a nice body and all that, but we had abducted her. It was hardly the way to make friends and influence people.

"I told you before, you're being ridiculous, Brenda," I said.

That's when she became totally unreasonable.

"You're just like all the other men, Matthew. All you want is to use a girl and then dump her."

Where she got that idea from I don't know, but she sounded very bitter.

"You're jumping to conclusions," I said, trying to reason with her, but instead of calming down, she became even more incensed. That's when she started ranting and raving about "men" and about her other boyfriends, who had also "betrayed" her, so in the end I just shut up and said nothing until she ran out of steam. All I can remember thinking is that she was becoming a real problem, that sooner or later she was going to say something to someone and let the cat out of the bag and get us both locked up. Eventually, of course, she calmed down, but the weekend was ruined before it had begun.

That was the day I decided that I was going to have to get rid of her, just like she'd got rid of Our Sarah and Rod. It wasn't something I wanted to do; of course, it was just something that had to be done. She was acting so crazy, she'd left me no choice in the matter.

On the Sunday morning, Mr Steadman, the owner made a surprise visit. It was the first time we'd seen him since we'd rented the farm, but I wondered how many times he'd been down to check the place out when we weren't there.

We had a brief chat out in the yard then he left again, but I was in a cold sweat all the time. I think I half expected the two bodies to push up from the ground and start calling out to him. After he'd gone Brenda had another go at me for being so jumpy. She said I'd give the game away if I didn't control myself better.

It was on the tip of my tongue to say, I'm not the problem, Brenda, you are, but I kept quiet. Sometimes, discretion is the better part of valour, if you know what I mean.

That evening Brenda apologised for being so short with me and we made it up in bed. The sex was really good, as good as anything we'd ever had, which only confirmed what I'd been thinking for some time – that she was completely unpredictable, like a bomb waiting to go off.

The next week seemed to go by in a blur. The newspapers were still full of stories about the missing girl, but the police seemed to be mystified by the entire episode. There was even talk that the Mafia or the Russians were involved, but it was all hot air, of course.

Most of the stories seemed to concentrate on Sarah and there wasn't too much said about the missing boyfriend at first, not until the reporters had said just about all they could about her, that is.

There had been some speculation at first that he was behind the kidnapping, out of jealousy or for the money, although no one was very clear about that particular detail. What was revealed though, was that he was a married man with a wife and a small son. According to one newspaper he had been separated from his wife for about eighteen months. She'd left him, the article said, after she found out about his philandering. What bothered me was the fact that there was now a young boy somewhere without a father.

When I showed the article to Brenda I watched all the colour drain out of her face.

"I didn't know he was married," she said in a very quiet voice.

I could see she was shocked about something. That's when I finally put two and two together.

"You knew him, didn't you?" I said.

She looked at me. For a long moment she didn't say anything.

"Yes, I knew him," she said in the end, but she wouldn't elaborate.

"Jesus Christ, Brenda," I said.

We had a lot of money now, but we couldn't really spend it. Of course, most nights we'd talk about where we could go and what we could buy, but it was only talk because we'd agreed that we weren't going to start spending for at least a year. And even then, we'd only use it for small purchases and a long way from home.

That's why I went mad a week later when I found out that Brenda had already been on a spending spree in the town.

It started as a small thing, really. We were watching TV at her flat. It had been ten days since the kidnapping when I noticed her wearing a pair of earrings that I'd never seen before. I didn't know if they were diamonds, but they looked expensive.

"You're wearing new earrings," I said.

She nodded. "Yes, that's right. I bought them last week."

I knew she was having trouble coming out on her salary from Thompsons because she complained about the "pittance" she was earning just about every other day.

"How did you pay for them?" I asked, even though I knew what she was going to say even before she answered.

"Cash," she said.

"What cash?"

"The robbery cash."

I was suddenly very angry, furious really. "Are you completely mad?" I asked.

"They only cost £100."

"What? We agreed that we'd not spend any more of the money

we've got hidden."

She shrugged again. "You said we could spend some when the time was right."

"Yes, when the time was right. Not now."

"Well I thought we'd waited long enough."

"It's only been a week," I said.

"Didn't you hear what I said? I used money from the robbery!"

It was obvious that she wasn't in the slightest bit concerned that she might have put the police on to us.

"The numbers might have been recorded."

"They're random numbers. We checked that too, remember. And the police officer who questioned you about the hijacking said that the money was untraceable."

"He might have been lying," I said.

What really bothered me was the fact that Brenda had suddenly decided to spend some of the money without asking me. It was the last straw.

"We had an agreement about this," I said.

"I didn't think that spending a bit would hurt. Anyway, it's only a small amount. It's not like I went out and bought a Ferrari."

"But it's the principle of the thing."

"I've said before, you're becoming paranoid, Matthew. If you're not careful you're going to give us away."

"And you're not paranoid enough," I answered.

She laughed at me then got up and went into kitchen to make us a sandwich. A moment later she was standing in the doorway, with the bread knife in her hand.

"I had a phone call today," she said, looking very serious. "My aunt's very sick. I might have to go and look after her."

"Oh," I said.

When I saw her standing there the thought had flashed through my mind that it would be easy to get up, grab the knife out of her hand, stab her in the heart and solve all my problems in one fell swoop.

I think she must have seen something in my face because she said, "What are you thinking about, Matthew?"

"You didn't tell me she was sick," I said, trying not to look too flustered.

136

"That's because I didn't know."

"So when are you planning to see her?"

"I think I'll have to go on Monday, after we get back from the farm-house.

That Friday was my last day at work and we'd planned to go away for the weekend again, to celebrate "my retirement", as Brenda called it.

"I think I may have to look after her for quite a long time," Brenda said.

"What does that mean?"

"It means she's got cancer. I may have to give up work."

"Have you told her what you're going to do," I said, "your aunt I mean."

"No, I haven't. It's going to be a surprise."

The next day, I heard Brenda telling the other girls that she'd applied for compassionate leave because she had to go and look after a sick relative and later on Mrs Williams visited her at her desk to offer her condolences.

I think that was when it struck me that it was the perfect opportunity to get rid of Brenda. For one thing her aunt's illness could take months to run its course, so no one would be surprised if she didn't come back to work, and for another she hadn't yet told her aunt what she was planning, so if I acted swiftly no one would miss her. Also, being as I was leaving too, I'd be able to do what I had to do and move on without anyone being the wiser. I have to say though, that deciding to kill her was a very difficult thing for me to do because I'm not by nature a violent person. But I knew I had to take the initiative to prevent a disaster from happening.

After drinks at work that Friday night, which Brenda had arranged because I was leaving, we went back to her flat, collected some things then drove out to the farmhouse.

I had an old golf club hidden in the boot of my car that I was planning to hide on the riverbank next to the graves somewhere, so it would be handy when needed.

Believe it or not, I felt very calm about the whole thing once I'd set my mind to it. That was partly because everything seemed to have fall-en so neatly into place and partly because I knew I had no choice. At the end of the day, Brenda had brought it on herself. She really had left me with no alternative.

BRENDA'S STORY

Monday 31 January

TODAY I STARTED a new job as a secretary with a firm called Thompsons Engineering. They make pipes – the sort that go in the ground, not the sort you smoke. I have a desk up one end of the typing pool, which is a big cavern of a room that the bosses call Secretarial. I suppose you could say that's the bad news, having to start work again, I mean. The good news is that I think I've seen Mr Right. His name's Matthew Woodgate.

The other girls think Matthew's strange. "Introverted" was how Jenny Martin, the head of typing described him, but I knew he was special from the first moment I laid eyes on him.

That was about two o'clock this afternoon. He was in his office, working at his computer and I was standing next to my desk. I'm not sure why I hadn't paid him any attention before, but that's probably because I'd been so busy, settling in and everything, and the fact that he hadn't been down to the canteen for lunch with the rest of us. Anyway, we both happened to look up at the same time, which is how our eyes came to meet. I was going to smile, but he looked away before I had a chance.

The first thing that struck me is how good-looking he is – high cheekbones, blue eyes, dark hair etc. – but it wasn't his looks that made an impression on me. It was something else, a special quality I sensed about him, a stillness I suppose you'd call it.

I remember thinking: he's The One, which sounds ridiculous considering I hadn't even spoken to him, but I sometimes get a feeling about these things. It's a kind of sixth sense I have.

I was surprised that none of the other girls liked him, even Jenny, who doesn't have a bad word to say about anyone. She says that he's "weird" and Gloria, the girl who sits next to me, says he has "delusions of grandeur," whatever that means. He likes to keep himself to himself, thank goodness, she said.

After that first brief encounter, the rest of the afternoon went by in a blur. I tried to look interested and enthusiastic being as it was my first day, but it was hard to concentrate after I'd seen Matthew.

Tuesday 1 February

I TRIED TO FIND OUT some more about Matthew today. Discreetly, mind you, no blatant questions, just showing a passing interest in my co-workers, that sort of thing. The girls reckon he's single and unattached, though no one's absolutely sure because he keeps himself to himself so much. Gloria says he's a loner and she calls him as Our Resident Mystery Man. It's just about all he can do to pass the time of day with us mere mortals, she says.

The interesting thing is that Jenny Martin reckons he knows exactly what people are saying about him, but that he doesn't care. I think that's a very refreshing attitude on his part because most people tend to do what everyone else wants them to do, but he's been able to resist that particular temptation, which says a lot about his strength of character, in my opinion.

He likes to keep himself apart, Jenny says. According to her, the only time he's been really agitated was when two of the girls had a bet on to see how long it would take to get him angry enough to lose his temper. To settle the argument they started talking dirty outside his office and Jenny said that some of the things they came out with even made her blush. It wasn't until the second day that he finally spoke up and objected "in the strongest terms" as he put it.

"That kind of gutter-style vulgarity is completely out of place in a working environment," he said, which Jenny admitted was perfectly true, although that wasn't the point. The point, she said, was that he'd reacted just like everyone had expected him to. Pompous, she called him, which I thought was a bit strong under the circumstances.

Despite what everyone says, I still can't understand why no one else is interested in him. After all, its not as if the place is brimming with eligible bachelors. Still, their loss is my gain.

Wednesday 2 February

I DIDN'T SEE MUCH of Matthew today because he was working over in the admin building most of the time. I only caught a glimpse of him at tea break in the afternoon. He had his head stuck in a book in his office, completely wrapped up in himself. I thought of going to ask him what he was reading, but managed to resist the temptation. We still haven't been formally introduced, you see, and I don't think it's my place to make the first move. After all, a respectable girl isn't supposed to be too willing and eager, is she?

Gloria asked me if I wanted to go out for a drink with her on Friday night and I said I would because I think she's desperate to be friends. I gather she's not that popular with the other girls, probably because she's a bit of a busybody and always sticking her nose into other people's affairs. For example, the first thing she asked me when we got to know each other a bit better was whether or not I had a boyfriend. I nearly told her to mind her own business, but I wasn't sure that would go down too well, me being the new girl and everything, so I said I was "in between relationships", although I didn't go into detail. I could have told her about my disappointment with P, that men are untrustworthy, that they only betray you in the end, but I resisted the temptation. She wouldn't have understood. And anyway, I prefer to keep my private life private.

Gloria says she's also "in between relationships" so she reckons we should make a good team.

Friday 4 February

THIS MORNING I HAD A FOLLOW-UP interview with Mrs Williams, the head of personnel. She wanted to know if I was settling in okay and that kind of thing.

"Everything's going very well, Mrs Williams," I said, which seemed to please her.

Gloria says she's a vindictive, stuck-up cow and that the less you have to do with her, the better, which is probably not far off the mark, if first impressions are anything to go by.

I didn't see much of Matthew again. He was hard at work in his office all day. Fridays are his busy time I'm told because he has to do the wages for the factory.

He walked past my desk twice this morning and both times I felt all fluttery inside. I have to say that I was disappointed that he didn't even glance at me, but I didn't let on.

The strange thing is I think he's interested in me despite the fact that we haven't even spoken to one another yet. Of course, I know from experience that men can be fickle creatures so for the time being I'll just let things simmer and wait and see how they turn out. I'm not going to push matters yet because Gloria says that Matthew's made it very clear in the past that he doesn't want anything to do with any of the office girls and the last thing I want to do is to scare him off before anything's even got started. Of course, I haven't told Gloria how I feel about Matthew because she'd think I was mad.

Maybe I am.

Apparently we're going to a place called The Palace tonight. I can't say I'm that enthusiastic, but being as I'm new in the district it will be good to have someone to show me around.

Monday 7 February

I SPOKE TO MATTHEW TODAY. I had to take him a letter to sign, but when I walked into his office he was so wrapped up in what he was doing he didn't notice me at first. That gave me a chance to have a look around. What struck me the most is how tidy he is. The whole place is a shrine to neatness and order. A place for everything and everything in its place. Not like my desk, which always looks like a bomb's hit it.

He's about six foot tall, which is perfect being as that's about two inches more than me. He usually wears a jacket and trousers with a white shirt and tie, never anything too trendy like jeans or a t-shirt, just ordinary clothes, so he's quite old fashioned really, though I don't mind that because I'm not one to go on appearances.

On Friday night Gloria told me that some of the girls think he's queer, but I said that I didn't think so. "That's just because he's what some people would call a nice young man," I said.

She laughed when I said that. "You fancy him, don't you?" she replied, but I answered that I was just being objective. "He's respectable," I said. "He's not a toucher or one to make crude remarks, which makes him different to all the other men in the factory." That's why some of the girls don't like him, because he's not the same as anyone else, which she agreed with after she'd given the idea some thought.

The thing that fascinates me about Matthew is how he keeps himself to himself all the time. I sometimes wonder if it's because he has a secret life that consumes all his interest or whether there's some other reason, like he's obsessively shy for example. I think that men who keep themselves to themselves like that usually have something to hide, which is one of the reasons I want to get to know him better, to find out all his secrets.

Gloria says that the more you get to know him, the more distant he becomes, which is a funny thing to say because things normally work the other way around. I think the main problem is that none of the other girls have taken the time to get to know him properly. I didn't say that to Gloria, of course, because if I had she'd have probably put two and two together and got four.

A lot of the girls can't understand why he has his head in a book all the time, but that's because they're illiterate. I don't mean that they can't read or write, I mean they're unacquainted with literature. People who read make them nervous because they're outsiders, like aliens from another planet who keep receiving coded messages all the time. Of course, about the only thing most of the girls ever read are the instructions on a bottle of nail varnish so it's not surprising that they get so suspicious and hot under the collar like they do. Mind you, having listened to them go on about things, I can understand why Matthew doesn't want anything to do with any of them and prefers to keep his own counsel.

When he saw me suddenly standing in front of his desk, he was quite shocked and I don't think he was very pleased about the fact that I had been able to creep up on him unawares, not that that was what I was trying to do.

"How long have you been standing there?" he asked very quietly.

He's got quite a posh voice, not coarse and common like the other men in the factory. It's like he's been to a public school or something, though I don't think he has.

"I've got something for you to sign," I said.

When I put the letter on his desk he just gave me a cold look, scribbled his name on the bottom and threw it back at me.

I still don't know why he was so upset. It might have been because I'd been able to catch him unawares, but it I think it was more that he was just embarrassed for some reason. He's a bit of a closed book at the moment so it's hard to tell.

I have to admit that it was hardly an auspicious first meeting, but it was interesting. I keep thinking about his eyes. They're a very pale blue, piercing, I suppose you'd call them, though he doesn't look at you most of the time.

When I got back to my desk Gloria wanted to know what he'd said to me. "He didn't say anything," I said, "he just signed the letter and chucked it back at me." From the way her expression changed I thought she was going to storm into his office and give him a piece of her mind, but in the end she just shrugged and went back to work. "He's just a miserable bastard," she said.

Gloria and I went to The Palace on Saturday. At the end of the night we got a lift home with two men she knew named Larry and Steve. Larry phoned her at work this morning and suggested that the four of us go out for a drink sometime this week and Gloria said yes without asking me. I was angry at being taken for granted and I told her so in no uncertain terms. After that she was all apologies and begged me to go along, so I agreed to go in the end, even though I'm not in the slightest interested.

Gloria hasn't said so, but I know she's got the hots for Larry.

Sunday 13 February

I DIDN'T SPEAK TO MATTHEW LAST WEEK. Once or twice I caught him staring at me, but when I met his eyes he looked away and pretended to be doing something else. That kind of behaviour makes me cross, acting like he hasn't seen me when we both know that he has, I mean. Sometimes I even think he's purposely avoiding me, hiding away in his office, like a recluse.

I find those kinds of silly boy/girl games very irritating, which is why I've played it cool for a few days – so that he realises that I'm different to the other girls.

Gloria, Larry, Steve and I went out to a pub on Wednesday night. I was bored out of my mind but Gloria couldn't keep her hands off Larry and the next day she kept saying what a good time she'd had, so it was obvious she didn't feel the same.

Last night (Saturday) the four of us went out to The Palace again. Afterwards Gloria went back to Larry's flat and Steve drove me back to the hotel where I'm staying. I let him kiss me goodnight and I think he was put out when I didn't invite him up to my room, but that's his problem not mine. I half expected him to start pawing at me, but he didn't try to push things, thank goodness.

He asked me if I wanted to go out for a drink with him again and I said yes although I shouldn't have done, but I was taking the line of least resistance. I could hardly say, "Look, Steve I'm really not interested because I have my sights set on someone else," now could I?

Monday 14 February

I WENT TO SPEAK TO MATTHEW after lunch today. It wasn't something I planned, more a spur-of-the-moment thing. Taking the initiative, I suppose you could call it.

When I was standing in front of him my mouth suddenly went very dry. That's when I nearly blurted out, "I've been waiting for you, Matthew," but the words wouldn't come. They made sense inside my head, but I knew they'd sound ridiculous said out loud.

"Why don't you ever eat in the canteen with the rest of us?" I said after a long and embarrassing pause.

I held my breath because my whole body was prickling with a kind of shivering excitement. I had my hands clasped to stop them from shaking and I wanted to reach out and touch his face, to feel his skin against my fingers, but I didn't, of course.

Instead of answering, he just stared at me. I don't think anyone has ever looked at me like that before. Really looked at me, I mean.

By the time he eventually got around to saying something I'd already lost my nerve and was running out of his office. I got back to my desk feeling completely foolish. To make matters worse, I was panting like a dog and Gloria, who had watched the whole thing, naturally thought Matthew had said something nasty to me. It was all I could do to stop her storming off into his office to give him a piece of her mind, but when I saw her at his desk an hour later I just knew she hadn't been able to resist the temptation to stick her nose into my affairs.

When she came back to her desk I was waiting for her. I was furious.

"You don't have to fight any battles for me, Gloria," I said sharply.

Suddenly, there was a shocked look on her face.

"I was just trying to be a good friend," she said.

We're not friends, you stupid interfering bitch, I thought, we just work together, but I didn't say that. I stayed very calm.

"That's very kind," I said coolly, "but I'm quite used to looking after myself."

That's when it finally dawned on her that she'd overstepped the mark.

"I'm sorry," she said, looking very downcast.

I decided to let it go at that because I didn't want to make a mountain out of a molehill as that would have just made things worse. I just knew I had to let her know what the ground rules were because I had no intention of letting anyone come between Matthew and me.

"It's okay" I said, like the whole thing was forgotten, pretending to forgive her.

Tuesday 15 February

GLORIA WENT TO SEE MATTHEW again this morning. To mend some bridges, she said. She stayed talking to him for about fifteen minutes. When I asked her what they had talked about, she said he'd showed her the book he was reading. It was about Superman, she said.

"You mean the Christopher Reeve Superman, the Hollywood Superman?" I asked.

"Yes," she said, which surprised me I have to admit. For some reason, I expected him to be reading something more serious.

Friday 18 February

I'VE HARDLY SPOKEN TO MATTHEW SINCE "the argument" on Monday. I purposely kept out of his way again for a few days, to let the dust settle, but yesterday, I saw him heading for the vending machine at the top of the stairs so I casually drifted over.

"How are you?" I asked, as if us bumping into each other was entirely accidental.

He looked quite startled when I spoke to him, almost like he wanted to run away.

"Fine, thank you," he said.

I was going to ask him about his Superman book, but he just picked up the bar of chocolate he'd bought and headed back for his desk without another word, which was a disappointment because I was hoping we'd get into a conversation. Unfortunately, that didn't happen, but at least we've re-established contact, which is about as much as I can expect at the moment given Gloria's interference.

I was tempted to explain to him that I just wanted to get to know him better, but I knew if I blurted something out again or said the wrong thing, that would probably be the end of it, so I played it cool and aloof instead.

Gloria's pestering me to go out with Steve again, but I keep putting her off. I don't want to tell her that I don't like him, that I'm only interested in Matthew because she would think I was mad. The irritating thing is that she keeps saying things like, "Steve's such a nice guy", or "Steve's got such a good job", as if things like that would make any difference. P also had a "good job" and look where that got me!

Since I moved north towards the end of last year I've been staying at a hotel, until I can find something more permanent. It's an extravagance I have to admit. I've been using the money I got from my dad's life assurance policy, but that's just about gone now. This morning there was an advert in the newspaper placed by someone who wants to share a flat. I phoned the girl as soon as I got to my desk and I'm going to see her this evening after work.

Sunday 20 February

I MOVED INTO A NEW FLAT this afternoon. Helen, the girl who has the lease, wants someone to help her pay the rent because her last flatmate got married and moved out at the end of last month. The apartment is on the top floor of a big house in a good part of town and the rent's quite reasonable. All things considered, I think I've been quite lucky.

I explained about moving to Gloria and gave that as a reason why I couldn't go out with her or Steve over the weekend. I said that I had a lot of organising to do, which sounded quite lame, but she didn't ask any questions. I think she's finally beginning to get the message.

Steve phoned me at work at lunchtime on Friday and left his number with the switchboard, even though I'd told him not to. I was so furious I phoned him back the minute I got the message and told him that I didn't want to see him again. Don't phone me at work again, I said. He started to apologise, but I just put the phone down on him.

A funny thing happened yesterday.

When I was putting away my things in my new bedroom I came across a stack of old news papers that the previous girl had left in the wardrobe. For no particular reason I started leafing through them and that's when I came across the photograph of P. His parents were offering £1 000 reward to anyone who knew where he was because he'd been missing for seven weeks.

It was funny seeing his picture again, but not half as distressing as I thought it would be. I expected to be quite upset, but the truth is I didn't feel a thing, which means I'm now completely over him.

I've decided not to get in touch with his mother or father. I couldn't claim the money anyway and too much time has passed. Also, there's nothing I want to tell them, apart from the fact that their son was a deceitful, unpleasant person.

Sunday 27 February

IT'S BEEN A QUIET WEEK.

I haven't seen much of Helen, my new flatmate. She was only at home on Wednesday and Thursday. Most of the time she stays at her boyfriend's place. I haven't met him yet, but I have seen his picture, which she was very proud to show me. I gather he's got a lot of money and comes from a "good" family, but I can't say I'm impressed.

The photograph she showed me had been taken at a restaurant. He was wearing jeans, a denim shirt and a bow tie and was grinning like a moron, but then what else can you expect from someone who uses a bow tie to make a fashion statement? He has big sticky-out ears, which his hair doesn't quite hide and what my mum used to call a weak chin. He looks totally gormless, a typical hooray-Henry.

Helen said that they were hoping to get married in September and that Ralph – her boyfriend – had promised to take her to Mauritius for their honeymoon.

That's very nice, I said, trying to look suitably impressed. I was pretending to be happy for her because she sounded so pleased with herself and I couldn't think of anything else to say.

That's when she said she was going to invite me to the wedding. From the look on her face you'd have thought she'd just offered me the secret of eternal youth.

"Lovely," I answered, trying not to look completely under-whelmed at the prospect. I could hardly say, I could think of nothing worse, Helen, which is what I was thinking.

If Matthew and I got married we'd go somewhere much more interesting than a tropical island for our honeymoon, darkest Africa or the North Pole, somewhere like that. Then we'd settle down in the country, where we'd buy a beautiful farmhouse to bring up our children. We'd be the perfect married couple.

I've hardly spoken to Matthew all week. Most days I have to go into his office, to take him a letter to sign or something like that, but we don't talk, not about anything that isn't work related, I mean. Even so, I think I'm beginning to understand him more, now that I'm getting to know him a bit better. He's a very intense person and he takes his job very seriously, which is probably why he doesn't have time for any of the girls, who are always joking and messing around, never putting their mind to things. Not that he's ever said anything to me about anyone at work, it's just an impression I've got. There are clues about how he's thinking though, if you know what to listen out for. On Tuesday, for example, I had to take him a letter that Gloria had typed.

When I put it on his desk, he stopped what he was doing and looked up at me.

"Have you checked it for mistakes?" he asked.

"No," I said, "I haven't."

" Then maybe you should."

I didn't know what to say and we both stood staring at each other until he reached out and pushed the letter at me. "Thank you," he said.

He'd been polite enough, but I didn't like his superior tone, like he was the master and I was the servant, and it was on the tip of my tongue to ask him who he thought he was, but I just picked the letter up again and went back to my desk instead.

I found four typos and a spelling mistake and I had to ask Gloria to do the whole thing again before I could take it back to him. Since then I've been checking the things she gives me to pass on and I've found that she's very slapdash work-wise, just as Matthew hinted.

"I shall try to be more careful in future," I said, when I took the letter back to him the next morning.

"Yes, that would be a good idea," he answered, but I could tell from the look on his face that he wasn't convinced. I could almost hear him saying, "I've heard it all before, Brenda, I've heard it all before", but I shall prove him wrong.

I realise that he's very meticulous about things so from now on I'm going to be extra-specially careful about any work I take him.

Monday 28 February

TODAY WAS FANTASTIC. A turning point!

What happened was that I had to take some work back to Matthew, but I'd purposely waited until lunchtime, when all the other girls had gone down to the canteen, before I went to see him. When I walked into his office he had his head buried in a book as usual.

After I'd put the folder down, I asked him what he was reading. There was a long pause before he answered and from the look on his face I thought I'd said the wrong thing. I was just about to apologise and say I was sorry for interrupting, when he said, I'm reading a book written by the Marquis de Sade.

I know all about de Sade and sadism and so on and I was about to say so when it suddenly struck me that men tend to be a lot more forthcoming if they can explain something to a "dumb" girl, so I decided to play the blonde and let him feel superior, which turned out to be the perfect strategy.

"Isn't a marquis a rich person?" I asked, like I was really interested.

That was when he launched into a long explanation about de Sade, his family and background and that kind of thing.

The book he was reading was called *One Hundred and Twenty Days of Sodom*, and was all about de Sade's experiences with a prostitute when he was locked up in prison. The book wasn't about sex, Matthew said, it was about relationships and power and control, which was stretching things a bit, if you ask me. Anyway, we spent about fifteen minutes talking about it, me playing the attentive student, him explaining, showing me how knowledgeable he was. After that I went back to my desk again.

As I said, I feel that was a turning point, us having a real conversation, I mean, but the strange thing is, while Matthew was talking, all I could think about was P. It was the blue and white shirt Matthew was wearing that did it. P had been wearing one exactly like it the last time I saw him. That was only six months ago, but it seems more like six years, which is why I was surprised that the memories came flooding back so vividly.

We'd bumped into each other in the food hall at Marks & Spencers. I was doing my grocery shopping and he was there to buy some socks. We had a chat next to the fresh produce counter then he offered to buy me a cup of coffee. Knowing him like I did, I was reluctant at first, but he could be very persuasive, when he wanted to be so in the end I agreed. Afterwards, he suggested we go for a walk down by the river.

When I said, "but aren't you supposed to be at work?" he looked around, very serious-like as if he thought someone might be watching us, then he burst out laughing.

"We'll just make it our little secret, shall we?" he whispered.

Later, after we'd parked the car and were walking towards the woods, we passed a fisherman and stopped to watch him pull a fish out of the water.

I remember how hard my heart was beating.

"I don't want you to leave me again," I said.

I hated being so weak, but I couldn't stop myself.

That's when he put his arms around me. I could feel his warm breath on my ear.

"I love you, Brenda," he whispered. "I'll always love you. You know that don't you?"

I knew he was lying, but I tried to convince myself that he really did mean it. That's why I went along with everything. Until the end, that is. He only has himself to blame for what happened in the end.

Monday 6 March

TODAY I FOUND OUT MATTHEW got turned down for the job of senior clerk. The fact that he'd even applied for the job was supposed to remain confidential, of course, but these things have a habit of getting out. Heather Clawson, Mrs Williams' assistant, first let the cat out of the bag a few days ago when she let slip that he'd applied for the job, and this morning there was a memo on the notice board announcing the name of the successful applicant.

I felt quite sorry for Matthew and I considered going to commiserate with him, but I wasn't sure how he'd take it, especially since I wasn't supposed to know that he'd applied for the job in the first place, so I didn't say anything and neither did he, though I thought he looked quite down in the dumps.

Friday 11 March

STEVE PHONED ME AT HOME on Wednesday night. He must have gotten the phone number from Gloria. He wanted to know if I'd go to a party with him at the weekend, but I turned him down, because I said I'd made other plans. That's when he started to get ratty so I reminded him that I'd already said that I didn't want to see him again, which is when he slammed the phone down on me.

I considered giving Gloria a piece of my mind about letting him have my phone number, but in the end I decided not to because I thought it might cause an argument, which could have made things unpleasant at work.

She was the one who brought the subject up the next day during morning tea break.

"I'm sorry you and Steven didn't hit it off," she said.

I shrugged, like it wasn't a big deal. "I don't think we're suited," I said. She didn't try to argue the point.

"Yes, you're right," she agreed. After a pause, she added, "but there's plenty more fish in the sea, I suppose."

"Yes, but who wants to go out with a fish," I said, making a joke of it.

We're still friendly, but we don't see much of each other after hours these days because she spends all her time with Larry. I gather she's thinking of moving in with him.

I've decided to keep out of Matthew's way (again!) as much as possible for the time being because I don't want him to think I'm trying to take advantage of our new-found friendship. I also want to keep him interested, by playing hard to get. There's also a third reason: one or two of the other girls have started spreading the rumour that we're having an affair or something. They know it's not true, of course, it's just their stupid idea of fun, but these things have a way of getting out of hand.

Yesterday, for example, I had to take a letter across to Mrs Williams' office, and I was unlucky enough to bump into her in the corridor.

"I'm sorry that your boyfriend didn't get the job of senior clerk, Brenda," she said, "but we had to employ the best person for the job."

I knew exactly what she was talking about, but I played dumb.

"I don't know what you mean, Mrs Williams," I said.

"Matthew," she said, "your boyfriend."

"He's not my boyfriend, Mrs Williams," I said. "We just work together, that's all."

She made a show of looking relieved, sighing like I'd suddenly taken a great weight off her shoulders.

"I'm pleased to hear that because you'd only be wasting your time on him, Brenda," she said. Then she closed her eyes in a kind of despairing disbelief.

"What gave him the impression he could run the finance department, is beyond me," she added, the cow.

I know a lot of people think Matthew's very strange but that's because they don't know him like I do. He has a very organised and methodical mind and he takes his job very seriously, which some people find quite threatening. I'm sure he would have made a really good senior clerk, but the problem is that he doesn't have the right interpersonal skills, as the human resources people like to say.

I wanted to say, if you knew Matthew like I do, Mrs Williams, you'd realise what a big mistake you're making, but I knew that wouldn't go down too well, so I walked away without saying anything.

Saturday 18 March

MATTHEW AND I BUMPED into each other today. It was the first time we've spoken to each other outside of work. It was quite by accident, really. I'd gone to visit my Aunt Mary who lives across town. She broke her hip about a year ago and nowadays she doesn't get around as well as she used to, which is why she asked me to take her dog for a walk.

It was while we were out walking that a bad thing happened: Merlin ran into the road and got hit by a car, which didn't stop. I should have been taking better care, I suppose, but I had other things on my mind and a stupid dog was the last thing I was interested in.

The dog just lay in the street after it had been knocked down. It was whimpering and there was blood around its mouth, so I knew it was badly hurt. I didn't know where the nearest vet was, which is how I

ended up running into Matthew: I went looking for the Peoples'
Dispensary for Sick Animals, which I thought was on Connaught road,
the other side of West Park.

I could tell straight away that he was embarrassed to see me, but I
guessed that was more because of his inexperience with women than
because he didn't like me. That's why I applied a bit of subtle pressure
and put on a scintillating display of girly weakness, which seemed to do
the trick because he offered to escort me to a vet he knew. Not that that
was such a great achievement because I think it's fairly easy for the
average woman to manipulate the average man. You just have to know
what makes the man tick, find the chink in his armour, so to speak,
which in Matthew's case seems to be doing whatever is most likely to
cause the least amount of disturbance to his routine.

After the vet, I played the helpless female again and got him to take
me for a cup of tea because I had no intention of letting the opportunity
to get to know him better slip past without a struggle. (And it was a
struggle, believe me!)

I don't think I've ever met anyone as reclusive as Matthew, which is
why the conversation in the café was such an effort to start with. Lots
of pregnant pauses and long silences, I mean. I knew he was reserved,
of course, but I thought that if I could get him alone and away from
work he'd loosen up. That was my first mistake! Getting him to talk
about himself was like drawing teeth. He admitted that he was a loner
and preferred his own company (surprise, surprise!), but to get him to
open up I had to pretend to hang onto his every word, like each sylla-
ble had been brought down from the Mount on tablets of stone.

When I first asked him about himself he became very suspicious,
like I was the enemy or something, which made me mad. I didn't show
it though I just backed off because I have to play the cunning bitch
where Matthew's concerned.

In the end about the only things I learnt were that he lives on his
own and didn't have a very pleasant childhood (who did?). Just about
everything else remains a mystery. He's like one of those funny little
Russian dolls, the ones that you open up and find an exact replica
inside. What you see is what you get with Matthew: you peel away a
layer and there he is again, only in a smaller version. The funny thing

is I find that kind of consistency quite appealing. It means there are fewer surprises in store for me.

After we went our separate ways, I had to go and tell Aunt Mary about Merlin. She was very upset as you'd expect, and insisted on telephoning the vet, not that he told her anything that I didn't.

Aunt Mary has always been good to me. When I was growing up she lived two streets away and I often used to go and visit her after school so we were always very close. After my mum died and my dad started getting more attentive, she was the only one I could turn to. Eventually, she had a big argument with him and he left me alone for a time. Then she had to move away and he started up again. We never talk about those times now, how she abandoned me, I mean, but I know she feels guilty.

It was my eleventh birthday, the day she left to come up north to start a new job. I went to see her off at the station. I remember us standing on the platform, both of us crying in the middle of all her suitcases. Eventually she stopped sniffling and gave me a hug. Then she held me at arm's length, the better to look at me.

Just remember one thing, Brenda, she said, men are animals, that's what they are – animals!

She was right; of course, men are animals – except for Matthew.

The trouble is, at one time I used to think P was different too. That was because he was so polite and considerate, but he proved a disappointment in the end, like most of the other men I've known.

The way we met was he used to come into the supermarket where I was working and we got chatting, then he asked me to go out with him.

He took me out for a meal on our first date, then we went back to his flat and got into bed. I loved him very much. I loved him right from the first day, but he took advantage of me, and when he'd got what he wanted he dropped me like a hot potato. That was when I found out he had a fiancée, that he was engaged to be married and that I was nothing more that a little distraction for him. He didn't know that I'd found out about his other life when he asked me to take a walk with him down by the river. I kept that particular piece of news for later on, for later on when I explained to him that there was a price to be paid for making a fool of me.

You have to pay for taking advantage, I told him. You have to pay just the same as my dad had to pay.

Monday 20 March

MATTHEW HARDLY SPOKE to me this morning, which was disappointing, given what happened on Saturday. I think he's afraid I'm going to start telling everyone that we have some kind of "relationship". I know because Gloria says he's made it very obvious he doesn't agree with "that kind of thing" at work, but I think it's the intimacy that bothers him. My guess is that he's never had a proper girlfriend before and he doesn't know what to do.

Anyway, I went to see him at lunchtime with the excuse that I had to tell him that Merlin had been put down. He pretended to be concerned, of course, but I could see straight through him.

When I started crying he looked very uncomfortable and began shuffling papers on his desk, like he wanted me out of his office. The strange thing is I think he quite likes me in his own strange way, but half the time he doesn't know how to react, which is why I have to take the lead – because he doesn't know how to.

At one point in the conversation when he was trying to explain himself, he said that he didn't believe it was right to mix business and pleasure.

"No, neither do I," I said, even though I didn't mean it, because I knew that was what he wanted to hear. The worst thing is I suspect he thinks I'm expecting him to take me out one night and ask me to marry him the next, which isn't what I want at all. That's not to say I don't dream about getting married, having kids, a house, that kind of thing, but all in good time. I'm not going to rush things.

Friday 24 March

ON TUESDAY I GAVE MATTHEW a bar of chocolate as a kind of thank-you gift for the vet incident, something to break the ice again, I suppose you could call it and afterwards we got talking. Now he's going to lend me some books to read. I think he thinks he's going to educate me in the ways of the world. Ha, ha! The other way around, more likely!

One or two of the girls in the typing pool think I've got a "thing" for him because I told them about him and Merlin and the vet, but I've made it very clear that there's nothing going on, that he's just someone I talk to, someone who reads books and has something interesting to say for a change.

This morning when I was in his office he asked me where I grew up.

"I moved here to be near my aunt at the end of last year," I said. "She hasn't been too well lately."

There was a silence. He looked at me across his desk, like he was deciding about something.

"What about your parents?"

I pretended to get weepy and upset, which definitely made him uncomfortable.

"My father died of cancer when I was eleven months old" – I should have been so lucky! – "and my mother drowned in a swimming pool a year later," I said. "After that I lived in an orphanage until I was sixteen."

I made out that I didn't want to talk about growing up, which is true, but not for the reason he thinks.

"You didn't live with your aunt, the one with the dog, I mean?"

"Aunt Mary isn't a real aunt," I said. "She was a friend of my mother who I just used to visit from time to time. But we were always very close," I added.

That bit of the story was true, well, partly at least, although after she moved north we didn't have much to do with each other apart from the odd letter, until I came here last year.

There was another long silence and Matthew was looking at me, but he wasn't seeing me.

"An aunt brought me up too," he said finally.

"I'm sorry to hear that," I said. "That you didn't grow up with your mum and dad, I mean."

He shrugged and gave a funny little smile, like it wasn't a big deal or anything, but I could see that it was.

"My Aunt Sal took care of me… when my mum ran off."

There had been a catch in his voice and I somehow knew that it was his aunt that he didn't want to talk about, not his mother.

"What happened to her? Your Aunt Sal, I mean."

He didn't answer, not properly anyway.

"I don't see her now," he said.

"At least we have something in common," I answered. "We've both been brought up by strangers."

"Yes, I suppose we have."

It was an automatic response because he wasn't thinking about what I'd said, he was thinking about Aunt Sal. And I could see her then. I could see her in his eyes: a thin, grey-haired old woman, bitter and twisted and vicious.

"Some people don't know how lucky they are," I said. Then I told him how I'd had to struggle to make something of myself after I left the orphanage. I laid it on thick just to get a bit of sympathy out of him. Not to make him feel sorry for me, mind you, because I don't want him feeling sorry for me, just so that he knows I'm not some kind of spoilt little rich girl, from the silver-spoon-in-the-mouth brigade, as he calls them.

"Ordinary people" – and by that he didn't mean either of us – "don't know what it's like just to have to survive every day," he said. Then he looked embarrassed, like he'd suddenly gone too far, said something he shouldn't have.

"I mean, sometimes we get pushed into doing things we don't want to, don't we?" he added.

He'd never said anything like that to me before.

"Yes," I said, "ordinary people, they aren't like us. They don't know they're born."

"Yes, you're right," he said smiling at me. (He has a lovely smile. It's a shame he doesn't use it more often.)

I'd never seen him look at me quite like that before – so kindly, I mean. That's when I knew that I really loved him, but I didn't say anything, even though I wanted to.

"I think I'd better get back to work," I said, then got up and went back to my desk.

The sane part of me knows it's ridiculous, the way I feel, I mean, but I can't help it. Falling in love is like catching a cold, it's not something you can control.

Saturday 25 March

I'VE BEEN THINKING about Matthew all morning. It was the conversation we had yesterday. We're not alike, it's more a case of opposites attract, but he's a very special individual and he has such an interesting view of the world, which is one of the things I like about him. To be honest, there are times when it crosses my mind that we're not entirely suited, but I don't pay too much attention because I know these kinds of fears are only to be expected under the circumstances, given my previous experiences with men.

Thursday 6 April

I READ WHAT I WROTE last weekend and I have to add that Matthew drives me crazy sometimes. Earlier this week, for example, he was moaning about his dead-end job and the fact that the bosses didn't appreciate his talents.

"Then why are you working here?" I asked. "Why are you doing this job? Why aren't you doing something more worthy of yourself?"

That's when he said he was waiting for the right opportunity to come along.

"You have to make your own opportunities," I said.

I was sharp with him, I suppose, but I couldn't help myself. I was infuriated because he is capable of much more.

He went quiet for a time then became all mysterious about his "Big Plans", but when I asked him what they were, he wouldn't say.

The truth is I'm not sure he has any "Big Plans", not real ones anyway. I think he said that just to impress me. He just has "Big Excuses" for not doing anything.

I suppose you could say that's the bad news. The good news is that things are finally looking up. Today Matthew asked me to go out with him at the weekend. It's some kind of film festival, he says. We've arranged to meet outside the cinema on Sunday afternoon.

Sunday 9 April

MATTHEW WAS LATE ARRIVING, but I knew he would be, so it wasn't as if it was a surprise or anything. I think he has these strange medieval ideas about women, that they need to be cosseted, controlled, kept on a short rein, that kind of thing. When I know him better, I'll have to explain the error of his ways to him.

What really struck me is how awkward he is with women. When we met outside the cinema I took his arm, which made him very uncomfortable, that much was obvious. He didn't quite know what to do and was actually quite flustered, though he pretended not to be. At first I thought it would be best if I kept my distance, then I decided it was his problem not mine and the sooner he got used to it, the better.

I expected the films – Matthew said they were something about Nazi propaganda – to be boring, but they weren't, they were really interesting and afterwards there was a panel discussion. I asked a question, but Matthew just kept quiet and I don't think he liked the fact that I'd spoken up and he hadn't. He didn't say anything but he had a kind of sulk on when we left the cinema.

Afterwards he offered to take me for a cup of tea, but I suggested we go to my place, which is what I'd planned we'd do all along. He wasn't too keen at first, probably because he was nervous, but he didn't put up too much resistance after I twisted his arm a bit. The thing is, I knew that if I left things to Matthew, we wouldn't have gotten anywhere, so in the end I took him off to bed, too.

Now I know he has no experience with women. He didn't have the foggiest idea what to do, so I had to take the lead, which was a new experience for me. Quite exciting really, being the dominant one. What I liked was the idea that I was the first and that he hasn't been poisoned by another relationship because that means he'll be mouldable, at least where the sex is concerned.

Monday 10 April

WHEN I GOT TO WORK this morning, there was a note from Matthew on my desk. He said that he thought it was a good idea that we keep our "relationship" secret, to avoid "wagging tongues" as he put it, which, as I said to him, was okay by me. Not that I had all that much choice. The most infuriating thing about Matthew is that he can't stand anyone expressing a different opinion about anything. When anyone disagrees with him all his insecurities start bubbling to the surface and he gets short-tempered and unpleasant. That's when he withdraws.

After work he came up to me and asked if he should come round to my flat later on, which is exactly what I'd expected him to do. That's because men seem to need their carnal pleasures a lot more than women, and a man once bitten – or sucked, as in this case – is usually hooked, at least until a better offer comes along.

Yes, of course, I said, which is when he turned and sauntered back to his office looking very pleased with himself.

That was when it struck me why Matthew keeps reminding me of P. P used to have the same self-satisfied expression on his face when he got what he wanted, too. That's why I sometimes can't help thinking that Matthew will end up treating me the same as P did, even though the two of them are complete opposites, P being a real charmer, I mean. Maybe that's just the cynic in me coming out, but I've been hurt before, and men being men, a girl simply has to look after her own best interests.

The day I let P talk me into going down by the river with him he said he wanted to "discuss our relationship", but that turned out to be just another lie. All he really wanted to do was get me into the woods and screw me up against a tree. And after he'd done that he suddenly discovered that he wasn't as keen for us to get back together again as he'd said he was. That made me feel dirty. Used.

"But you said you loved me," I said.

He laughed then, like the whole thing had just been a big joke. He only got serious when he saw how upset I was.

"It was just a bit of fun, Bren. You mustn't take these things to heart."

"It wasn't "just a bit of fun" for me," I said.

He was zipping himself up, checking for his car keys, not even looking at me. "You'll get over it," he said.

That was when I saw red, which is why I didn't let him just walk away like he was planning to do, not after the way he'd just treated me.

Wednesday 12 April

TONIGHT WHEN I GOT BACK to my flat after work, I cooked a special supper for us – chicken, roast potatoes, peas, the whole works and made a special effort and had everything ready for half past seven, which is the time Matthew was supposed to come round. He turned up at nine o'clock, when everything was ruined. He also said that he'd already eaten so I had wasted my time and got myself into a cooking tizzy all for nothing.

After I'd told him off for being late he got down to business and screwed me on the sofa, which was dangerous in a way because Helen, my flatmate, could have come back at any time, which made everything all the more exciting. The sex wasn't much better than the first time, since all he was interested in was pleasing himself, but I pretended he was the best lover in the world.

Afterwards, when he was getting ready to leave, I told him that I didn't like the way he ignored me at work. I made it clear that I wasn't suggesting we "go public" as he called it, merely that I wanted more respect.

"I don't ignore you," he said, "I just want to keep our relationship on a strictly professional basis at work. If we don't do that all the others will be spending every tea break talking about us."

I think he was quite shocked that I'd confronted him like I had, so I didn't try to argue the point, even though I wanted to tell him he was very self-centred at times.

Sometimes I'm amazed how he can justify everything in his own terms without even so much as batting an eyelid. That may be because he doesn't love me yet, at least not like I love him, but I'm sure that's just a temporary situation, a matter of time before I bring him around to my way of thinking and we become the perfect couple.

Sunday 16 April

MATTHEW HAS BEEN to see me three times this week. We always end up having sex and last night he stayed over. Fortunately, I haven't seen my flatmate for a week, though I think she's been home once or twice while I was out at work because I notice things have been moved in the kitchen.

Of course, he's easy to control now there's sex happening. It's a bit like leading him around by the nose, except it's not his nose we're talking about. Last night he asked me about my family again, and I made up some more "details". My father was a barrister, I told him, and highly respected in his profession. It sounded a lot better than telling the truth, that he was a delivery man, a drunkard and a womaniser. I didn't bother mentioning that the last time I'd seen him he'd tried to paw me again. That was eighteen months ago and he'd ended up in a heap at the bottom of the stairs with his neck twisted. Accidental death while under the influence of alcohol was how the inquiry described it. It was only the "accidental" part they got wrong.

It had started when I was ten, the year after my mum died. By that time I was the woman of the house doing the cleaning and cooking, making sure my dad had a meal on the table when he came home from the pub.

It was about six months after the funeral that I began to notice he was becoming more attentive. First he began resting his arm in my lap when we were sitting in front of the TV, then there were the small strokes along my legs, or playful pats on my bottom when I walked past him. Small, uncomfortable things, things I tried to tell myself that all fathers did to their daughters. Then his "touchings" became more intimate and I tried to avoid him, to stay out of his way in the kitchen or the garden, but he would come to find me and make an excuse for me to go into the house with him.

Then one night I woke up and found him in his pyjamas next to my bed. When I asked him what was wrong, he didn't answer at first. His hand was resting on the bedspread and there was a look in his face I'd never seen before.

"It is time for you to take the place of your mother," he said finally.

"I'm doing the best I can about the cooking," I began because he'd taken to complaining about the food a lot, but he shook his head, interrupting me.

"It's a daughter's responsibility to see to her father's happiness," he said.

"Yes, father," I said, though I didn't really know what he meant.

That's when he smiled at me and pulled back the bed coverings.

When I tried to drag the blankets back he caught my hand, crushing it in his fist until I let go again.

"A daughter has a duty to her father," he said sharply and lay down next to me.

After that he started coming to my bed regularly, once or twice a week at least, usually when the beer was in him, until I was fifteen and I could leave home for good.

I never spoke to him for nearly three years after that, until my eighteenth birthday when I went back to see him because I wanted some pictures of my mum that he had.

He was drunk of course. When I told him why I was there, he just smiled and pointed up the stairs. "They're in the bedroom," he said, but it was just a ploy.

When he tried to put his hands on me at the top of the stairs I turned and gave him a shove. For one frozen moment he seemed to hang suspended on the top step, then, raising his arms high in the air, like a high diver beginning a difficult routine, he began to tumble backwards.

He came to rest on the bottom step, his head on the floor, one arm twisted back at an unnatural angle. His eyes fluttered, opened slowly and focused with difficulty.

"Let me help you, daddy," I said, then I fetched a small side table from the living room and brought it down on his head.

Afterwards I called the doctor, who called the police and they asked me questions, but in a desultory kind of way. "He struck his head against the hall table when he fell," I said.

It was all very sad, everyone agreed.

Friday 21 April

Last night, MATTHEW WANTED TO KNOW ABOUT MY BOYFRIENDS, THOUGH he didn't say as much, not in so many words anyway, so I made up some stories to keep him happy, about how vulnerable I am and how I've been hurt in love, that kind of thing, which is what men like to hear because it makes them feel strong and in control.

What also happened this week is that he came up with what I initially thought was a hare-brained scheme to rob the company. At first I assumed it was all to do with the fact that he'd been turned down for the job of senior clerk, but I think I was wrong about that, too.

How it happened was that we were in his office and he started going on about how he'd been 'passed over' for promotion so I said he should look for a better job. The next thing I know he's talking about "doing something for himself", but when I asked him what he meant he became evasive.

"Matthew, you're not making any sense," I said, which is when he said that he was talking about making a lot of money.

"You mean like robbing a bank," I said, thinking I'd pull his leg a bit.

"Yes," he answered.

That was when I decided he'd gone off his head, but I had second thoughts later on when he explained what he had in mind, how he'd been watching the wages van, how lax the security was and how, if he had a set of ignition keys, he could just stroll over and drive it away before anyone had a chance to stop him. He'd got the whole thing worked out. It was amazing.

I didn't think it was going to be quite as simple as he described, but I was impressed, I have to admit that. Of course, the idea of hijacking the wages van is completely ridiculous, but it would be an exciting thing to do and he does have a plan that sounds almost good enough to work, so I've decided to play along for a while.

I can't help thinking that I've underestimated Matthew.

Saturday 22 April

LAST NIGHT we went over Matthew's plan again, but I still can't believe we're actually having serious conversations about pulling off a wages heist. What's even more incredible is that not only has he been thinking about doing the job for ages, but he's also "looked into the logistics" as he puts it, of carrying out a bank robbery! He's put that idea on hold for the time being, he says.

Wow!!!

It's all part of this Nietzsche/Superman idea he goes on about from time to time, superior people taking the initiative, that sort of thing. I still think he's (we're?) mad, but it's exciting. I mean who wouldn't like to hijack a wages van or rob a bank?

At first, all I could think about was what would happen if we got caught, but Matthew says it's just a calculated risk, which makes it seem like a big adventure. And he's thought about everything, right down to the last detail, so it wouldn't be as if we were going off half-cocked, or anything like that.

There's also the money to think about. Matthew reckons that the wages truck might be carrying over two hundred thousand pounds. I keep thinking about what I could do with that kind of money, how I wouldn't have to work at a crappy place like Thompsons any more. Matthew and I could go away together, too. A holiday somewhere exotic, then buy a nice house and settle down.

Everything's turning out to be perfect, just like I thought it would. I love Matthew all over again. All I hope is that we love each other all our lives and get married and live happily ever after.

Sunday 30 April

WE'VE BEEN GOING over the hijack plan all weekend. At first I thought the idea was completely insane, even though I went along with it, but not any more. Now I think there's a really good chance we can get away with it. The only problem is Matthew, who's become completely obsessed with the whole thing. He wants to go over "details" all the time. Sometimes he sounds like a stuck record, but it's in his nature to be very meticulous and he's better at that kind of thing than I am, so I try not to say too much.

Yesterday morning, for example, he was going over "The Plan" as he calls it, about how we were going to make the wages van break down and get a set of keys and all of that, but I couldn't concentrate. It was like I was in a dream. All I could think was: "This can't be real", then in the mirror I saw the two of us sitting across the coffee table from each other, and I knew that it was.

It's such a simple plan it's brilliant. The more he explains things to me, the more I understand why I love him so much.

Monday 1 May

LAST NIGHT I DROVE Matthew and a can of oil across town and dropped him off about half a mile from the security firm. He was away for about twenty minutes and I thought I was going to have a heart attack waiting for him. When he got back in the car he was excited, but a lot calmer than I expected him to be.

"Well," I said.

He was grinning from ear to ear. I'd never seen him so happy before. "Smooth as silk," he said, "smooth as silk."

This morning, he took a couple of hours of "personal time" at work so he could follow the wages van and wait for it to break down. He got back to work at eleven o'clock and I could tell from the look on his face that the news was bad, even before he said anything.

"Nothing happened," he said, when we finally got a chance to talk.

I was disappointed, but he was more jittery than disappointed. The least little sound was likely to make him jump. Last night he seemed strong and in control, which is something I admire, but he looked weak and pathetic this morning, and all because he'd had one minor setback. I think it's because his ego's so fragile: it's likely to fracture at the slightest touch.

"You have to have to get a grip on yourself, otherwise someone's going to notice," I said, when I took him a letter to sign later that afternoon.

He didn't say anything, but the look he gave me was pure venom. It was like I was looking at the old Matthew, the one I'd first encountered when I came to Thompsons.

I kept out of his way after that and by the end of the day, he'd calmed down.

He says he's going to break into the security firm again tonight and try something else.

Sunday 14 May

LAST FRIDAY WE HIJACKED the wages truck and stole £328 000.

To say it's been an exciting week is probably the understatement of the year. After the oil-in-the-petrol scheme failed, Matthew tried water, which worked. The wages van broke down almost as soon as it left the depot. That afternoon we visited the garage where it was being repaired. While Matthew chatted to the workshop manager about having his car serviced, I wandered around the workshop, very casually, like I had an interest in what was going on. I strolled over to the wages van and then walked around it. Someone had kindly left the door open so all I had to do was put my hand in and lift the keys out. We had copies made, then I put them back the next morning. It was all very smooth and simple, but I don't think I've ever been so scared in my life.

The next thing we had to do was organise some disguises. We decided it would be best if I dressed up like a man and Matthew went casual, jeans and T-shirt, that kind of thing. We were both going to wear wigs and false beards, which we got from a joke shop in the town.

Neither of us was going to win any beauty competitions, but they were effective all the same. Even our own mothers wouldn't have recognised us.

When everything was ready, we set the date.

On Friday we both phoned work very early. I said I had to go to the doctor and Matthew said that he had to have a puncture fixed. We met in the Mall and drove out to the security van depot in Matthew's car, which had on false number plates. After that it was just a case of following the wages van when it left on its delivery run.

The plan was that we'd hijack the van at a firm named Broads, but that didn't work because the driver and his mate didn't stay in the building long enough. Matthew had time to get out of the car though, but I knew he'd lost his nerve when I saw his face when he got back in again. He wanted to drop the whole thing and try again next week, but I wasn't going to put up with that so I took the lead.

At the next stop I just did the job myself: strolled over to the wages van, opened the door, started the engine and drove it away almost before anyone had the chance to notice.

After that we drove to a car park, transferred the cash boxes to the boot of Matthew's car and then went back to work. It really was quite simple and straightforward, easier than either of us expected I suppose you could say. The only disappointment was Matthew, who'd let us both down, not that either of us said as much. The last thing I wanted to talk about when the job was done was his pathetic inadequacies.

We smashed opened the boxes in the kitchen at Matthew's flat this evening. I've never seen so much money in my life. The place was swimming in bank notes. It was fantastic. I was all for going on a bit of spending spree straight away, but Matthew was adamant that we had to "stick to the plan" and "keep a low profile" for a time, whatever that means. I didn't mean that we should go and blow it all in Harrods, just that we could buy a couple of things we needed. Of course, Mr High-and-Mighty wouldn't even consider it, which is when I lost my temper. It was on the tip of my tongue to remind him who had actually stolen the money, but then I calmed down because I knew we both needed to keep a cool head for the next few days.

After that, we put it into two holdalls. Matthew's going to keep one and I'll keep the other.

Last night we counted the money again and arranged it all in small, neat stacks of £1000 each. From now on I'm going to count all the money in my holdall every night before I go to sleep, just to touch it.

Friday 19 May

LAST MONDAY WAS THE WORST. It was exciting to get back to work and find that the robbery was the talk of the place, but it was nerve-racking too. Once or twice, when I heard people talking, I'd butt in to the conversation and say something like, "The police think it was the work of expert professionals" just to see what the reaction would be. Usually everyone would nod and agree, but one or two people even complimented the robbers, saying what a good job they'd done. No one seemed to have any sympathy for any of the firms that had had all their money stolen.

As you'd expect, the police have been at Thompsons all week and they've questioned quite a few members of staff, including Matthew, but no one's been to see me. When anyone talks about the robbery I plead ignorance, like everyone else, which is probably why I've been ignored, but Matthew, who has a more intimate knowledge of the pay-roll deliveries because of his job, had a proper interview, although I think that was just a formality. He says the detective who interviewed him let slip that the police haven't got a clue. The policewoman I asked about the robbery didn't seem all that interested either.

I don't think the police have been very thorough, but they don't have that much to go on because it seems that we didn't leave that many clues behind us. We only found this out later. Someone had seen our car, of course, and the police knew the colour, but they'd got the make wrong and no one got the registration number. (When I first discovered that the police knew about the car I went into a state of panic for half an hour, but it turned out to be a lot of fuss about nothing in the end.)

Of course, it's very exciting knowing something that no one else does, but it's scary too because there's no way of knowing what clues might still turn up to give us away. That's why I'm glad now that I did what Matthew said and didn't go off and spend any of the money. I'd hate to think I might have drawn attention to myself, even in a small way.

There's no doubt that Matthew did a good job planning the whole thing, which is why the hijacking went off like clockwork, even if he did get cold feet at the very end. In that regard, I'm not angry with him any longer, more disillusioned I suppose you could call it, like finding that something you'd thought was the genuine article, turned out to be a fake. I still love him, I know that, but he can be very infuriating at times, especially his insistence on making all the decisions for us both. My father also used to like making decisions for me, and look where that got him. Anyway, I suppose the main thing is that the police are looking for a gang of "professionals" and not a couple of ordinary workers, which is all that matters in the end.

Friday 26 May

IT'S BEEN TWO WEEKS since the robbery and we still haven't been locked up and according to Mrs Williams, who has a friend who works in the Murder & Robbery Division, the police still don't have a clue.

Now that all the initial excitement has worn off, Matthew's gone back to his old tricks: he seems to think he has some God-given right to make all the decisions and tell me what to do. This morning, for example, I went into his office and said that I wanted to go and buy myself something with some of the money we'd stolen. I wasn't really serious, I just wanted to rattle his cage because he's become so over-bearing lately. He thinks he's some kind of super criminal who's carried out the perfect crime. The fact that he wouldn't have got anywhere without my help seems to have escaped him. He has a very short memory where his own shortcomings are concerned, does Matthew.

"Look, Matthew," I said when I saw the look he was giving me, "I'm an adult, I can make up my own mind, and it's not going to hurt anyone if I have a new pair of earrings or something."

"That's just being stupid," he said.

"No, it's you that's being stupid," I answered back.

I know it wasn't the right thing to say, but he'd made me angry.

"The money's off-limits," he whispered, like he was speaking to a child. "That's to keep us away from temptation."

What he really meant was that the money was off-limits to keep me away from temptation.

Sometimes I have a very short fuse and this morning was one of them.

"Don't patronise me, you arrogant bastard," I hissed.

He closed his eyes and actually counted to ten in front of me.

"If you don't want me to treat you like a child then you'll have to start acting like an adult, won't you, Brenda," he said finally.

For a second I saw red. I swear that if I'd had a gun in my hand at that moment, I'd have put a bullet between his eyes and wouldn't have felt a thing.

"You make me sick sometimes," I said and walked away.

Sometimes, when I think of Matthew, I can see the sharp planes of his face very clearly, his dark eyebrows and cool stare, then at others he seems to slip out of focus, like a blurred photograph. He portrays himself as a man of reserve and control, which he is, but there's another side to him too, an intolerant side that's small-minded and vindictive, like a spoilt child denied.

Saturday 27 May

MATTHEW'S TALKING ABOUT doing something else, robbing a bank, holding up a train, that sort of thing, but I don't believe he's serious because I think he's lost his nerve. Anyway, I've decided it's time we moved on a bit. Do something new and exciting, I mean – a kidnapping maybe.

The idea came to me about a week ago. What triggered it was a copy of the local newspaper. In the High Society section there was a feature about an art gallery opening. There were pictures of some local "celebrities" including one of a girl named Sarah Fitzgibbon.

"Miss Sarah Fitzgibbon and friend attended the celebration", the caption said.

The moment I saw the photograph it set my heart racing, but it wasn't the girl that got my attention, it was the man she was with. He was dressed in a tuxedo and his hair was slicked back in a way I'd never seen before, but I would have recognised him anywhere – Rod Bowers.

I remember the first time we met as clearly as if it was yesterday. That was last November when he came into the hotel where I was staying. He was standing in the lobby when I walked out of the restaurant after breakfast. He was there to see the manager about some loose roofing tiles. Later on I found out he ran his own business called Bowers Roofing Contractors.

He walked over to me and held out his hand. "I'm here for my appointment with Mr Davidson," he said, like that would explain everything.

Although I was flustered, I shook hands with him, because that was the polite thing to do, but I had no idea what he was talking about. I think he could tell that from the look on my face.

He hesitated, tilting his head inquisitively to one side in a way that I found quite attractive, but then he's very good at that, playing the innocent, making you like him, is Rod.

"You are Susan, Mr Davidson's secretary, aren't you?" he asked with exaggerated concern.

"I'm just one of the guests," I said.

"Oh, I'm sorry."

He was still apologising when the manager walked out of his private rooms behind the reception desk. We all laughed when he explained his mistake to Mr Davidson, then the two men went outside together to look at the roof.

I thought no more about the incident until I answered a knock on my bedroom door early that evening. Rod was standing in the corridor with a big bunch of flowers in his arms.

"To apologise for this morning's embarrassing mistake," he said, holding them out to me.

When he smiled, I felt my heart melt.

"There was really no need," I stammered.

I took the flowers, held the blossoms to my nose to smell the fragrance, more to hide my awkwardness than anything else.

He shrugged like it was no big deal, then turned to go. Ridiculously, I wanted him to stay, and talk.

"Thank you," I said, as he walked away.

That's when he turned around. There was silence for a moment before he said, "Will you have a drink with me tomorrow?" It was like he had spoken on a whim, like the thought had occurred to him suddenly and out of the blue.

"Yes," I said.

"About seven?"

"Yes."

Then he was gone and I was left standing in the doorway, still clutching the flowers, crushing them almost.

The next night we met in the town centre rather than at the hotel because he thought it best if the hotel manager didn't know about us. "I don't want him getting the impression I make a habit of this," he said, which I could understand.

He took me to a small restaurant called La Poisson, which was about three quarters of an hour's drive away.

"This place serves the best fish in the British Isles," he said, then ordered champagne to go with the meal.

Afterwards we went to a jazz club, a dark place underground somewhere, then at 11 o'clock he brought me back to the hotel, and pulled up in a side street.

"I enjoyed myself tonight," he said, when I was about to get out of the car.

"Yes, so did I."

"Then perhaps we can do it again sometime?"

"I'd like that," I answered.

Still the perfect gentleman, he leant across and touched his lips to my cheek. "I'll phone you," he said.

I wanted a more definite arrangement, a time and a place, something to look forward to, but I didn't think I could say that to him.

"Yes," I said.

The next time we spoke was a week later, when I'd just about given up hope of ever hearing from him again.

"I expected you to phone last week," I said.

"I'm sorry. I've been rushed off my feet at work."

I wanted him to explain properly, to give me a real reason, but all he said was, "Can I make it up to you?"

I thought of slamming the phone down on him, but I didn't.

"Yes," I said after a long pause.

That was when he brightened. "Good," he said. "Tomorrow? Same place – same time?"

"Tomorrow," I repeated, "same place, same time."

I arrived half an hour early and he arrived half an hour late. When at first I refused to forgive him, he pressed my hand to his lips, and planted four dainty kisses on my knuckles and that made my legs go weak. In another man that kind of thing would have seemed silly and overdone, but with Rod it was natural and perfect.

"To make it up to you, I shall take you dancing tonight," he said.

The club he took me to was an hour's drive away, but then we always drove far out of town.

"It's good to see you again, Mr Bowers," the maître'd said and led us to a table near the band. Later, Rod made my head spin as he swirled me around the dance floor.

That night he gently kissed me on the lips as we sat in his car outside the dance club.

"Thank you for a wonderful evening," he said.

He started the engine and drove me home, even though I would have been happy to stay there with him forever. But that was because I was already half in love.

Rod was very good at getting his way. When he was late, which was most of the time, he blamed work, a business meeting, a difficult client or a thousand-and-one other reasons. There was always a plausible excuse and sometimes even flowers or chocolates to repair the damage. His work was unpredictable, he said, and there had been hard times in the past.

It was a month to the day that he told me he loved me and I was in seventh heaven. That was when he first sneaked up to my room, using a back entrance to the hotel. He came to visit me more often after that, for a time at least. Then the excuses started again, a late meeting here, a job deadline there, then one evening after he had cancelled a date at the last moment, I spotted him going into a cinema with Sarah Fitzgibbon, though I didn't know her name at the time. He had his arm around her waist and she was leaning against him, just like I liked to do.

The next time he came to see me I confronted him, told him what I'd seen.

"You were supposed to be with me," I shouted.

He gave me a look I couldn't fathom then went and stared out of the window.

"You lied to me. You said you had to work."

Surprised almost, he turned to stare at me across the bed.

"So?"

He sounded amused almost, but his voice wasn't, it was icy cold.

"How could you?" I asked.

"How could I what?"

"Treat me the way you did!"

He had to think about this for a moment, consider his answer most carefully.

"You have to realise that my world doesn't revolve around you, Brenda," he said contemptuously.

I felt like I'd been stabbed through the heart. I was so shocked I couldn't speak even.

He collected his coat from the bed and headed for the door, where he paused for a moment.

"I suppose I should say it's been fun," he said, "but the truth is, it hasn't. You're too clingy for that," he said harshly, "too clingy by half."

Anyway, when I saw his picture in the paper all my old anger swept over me and I wanted to get back at him, trash his apartment, damage his car that sort of thing, but that was a silly idea. I had no idea where he lived and the effort, in all probability, would completely outweigh the returns. But I thought about nothing else for days. Then I wanted to kill him, then I wanted to kill her and make the police think he did it; put together a diabolical plan that would make him look guilty. Kill two birds with one stone, which is how I came around to the idea of a kidnapping. And then it struck me: kidnap him and I make him suffer, kidnap her and they both do.

Like I said, I planted the seed at my flat last night. Matthew and I were in the lounge, watching the news. There was a story about a businessman being kidnapped in South Africa by some Nigerians.

"I think they'll get away with it," I said.

Matthew gave me one of his condescending smiles.

"No, I don't think so, Brenda."

"Why not?"

"Because most kidnappers are stupid. Abducting the person is easy, it's getting hold of the money without getting caught, that's the hard part. That's the part that needs careful thought and planning."

"Yes, but you could do it, couldn't you? "

"Maybe," he said, going back to his paper.

He wasn't interested, the idea was a non-starter, I thought, deflated.

Five minutes later he turned to look at me. "If we wanted to kidnap someone we'd have to pick a person who has a lot of money, but who isn't high profile with a lot of bodyguards," he said.

"Yes, you're right," I agreed.

I thought for a moment that I'd given the game away by being too eager because he threw me a suspicious glance. Then he said, "The main question is, who would we kidnap?"

This time I played it cool.

"I don't know. Maybe we can find someone."

From the look he gave me I could see he still wasn't convinced.

Sunday 28 May

THIS AFTERNOON I SHOWED Matthew the picture of Sarah Fitzgibbon, even though I don't have a definite plan in mind. All I know is that a user like Rod needs to be taught a lesson because he can't be allowed to take advantage of innocent girls and just get away with it. And our Ms Fitzgibbon needs to be taught a lesson too! I hate girls like her, empty-headed girls who use their looks and money to get what they want, not caring about anyone else's feelings.

Anyway, when first I put the newspaper under Matthew's nose he made a point of not showing much interest, but I think that was more for my benefit than anything else.

"I suppose she might be someone we could consider," he said later on, after he'd studied her picture for a long time, but he didn't sound very enthusiastic.

It was hardly what you'd call an overwhelming vote of confidence for the idea, but I wasn't going to let a little thing like a touch of apathy put me off.

I pretended to be as indifferent as he was.

What if I try to find out something about her?" I asked, like the thought had suddenly occurred to me.

Matthew just shrugged. "Do whatever you want," he said.

It's clear that I've still got a lot of work to do to bring him around to my way of thinking.

Wednesday 31 May

I THINK MATTHEW likes the idea of abducting someone and having him or her completely in his power. He seems more enthusiastic about the idea now he's had chance to think about it. He hasn't said so, but then he's not one to show enthusiasm about anything. (Maybe he reckons that staying "cool" about everything adds to his air of mystery? It doesn't!) He probably has wet dreams about being in control and telling people what to do all the time. God help us all, if he ever becomes one of the bosses at work.

Yesterday, when I casually mentioned Our Sarah, he didn't seem interested, but today, quite out of the blue, he started raising all sorts of difficulties – where would we keep her, how were we going to get hold of the ransom money and so on – so something's changed.

Maybe something I said finally got through to him? Not that we're out of the woods, mind you, because now he's come up with a list of questions that he says we have to go through. It's a bit like a school test.

"I'm not going ahead with anything unless all our ducks are in a row," he said, very patronisingly. To hear him talk you'd think he was the only one who had any say in the matter.

"Absolutely," I answered, which made him look even more self-satisfied.

There are times when I get really angry when he speaks to me like that, like I'm a child, but I don't make a fuss because I know that's just the way he is. And anyway, whenever I get too insistent, I just see the shutters come down. That's why I'm using gentle persuasion to bring him around to my way of thinking, so that he thinks that whatever we do was actually his idea in the first place. I have to keep giving him a lot of little shoves in the right direction, not one big push. It's a bit like chipping away at a boulder, one tiny fragment at a time.

The worst thing is he's become very superior lately. Not in an obvious way, but in the way he talks about other people, like everyone's beneath him, not fit to kiss his feet, that sort of thing. He always had an arrogant streak in him, but now it's much worse. It's having all that money, I suppose. And he's dropped hints about giving up his job and going to live somewhere else, which he's never mentioned before.

I think he's going through a mid-life crisis twenty years too soon. Either that or he's finally growing up, twenty years too late!

Sunday 4 June

THIS MORNING I showed Matthew some more pictures of Our Sarah, as I've started calling her, and I made a big thing of emphasising how rich her father is.

"She's the perfect choice, Matthew," I said. "It'd be like taking sweets from a baby," I added, but I didn't overdo the enthusiasm bit, because I knew that wouldn't work with him.

"It won't be that easy," he snapped back, like he was speaking to an imbecile, but I considered that a victory of sorts. He could have said, "She's a lousy choice, Brenda", or "I've changed my mind, I'm not going through with it," which would have been a lot worse.

One of the things in my favour is the fact that Our Sarah comes from a wealthy home. Matthew resents with a passion anyone with a bit of money, the "landed gentry", as he's fond of calling them.

That's when I asked him if she was the sort of girl he thought we should kidnap.

He didn't answer straight away, like he was giving the question careful thought.

"She's a possible candidate, I suppose," he replied, after a long pause.

"That's what I think," I said.

The fact is I know she's the perfect choice, but I also know I have to give Matthew the chance to voice his reservations about any idea I come up with. That's because he always insists on pointing out my failings:

it's one of the little tricks he uses to keep me in my place.

The truth is, he's nervous. He's alright at planning things, living in his unreal world, but actually doing something concrete, acting on those plans, now that's something else. He proved that when he let us down during the cash robbery.

Sometimes Matthew can be all mouth and trousers, as my dear departed father used to say.

Later on, he started raising objections again, so I just played along, agreeing with him all the time, saying they were real concerns that we had to investigate before we did anything. In the end just by showing so much interest he painted himself into a corner and there was nothing he could do but agree to take another step forward, which is all I was hoping for.

He thinks that if he humours me enough, I'll probably get bored and give up the entire idea, which just goes to show how little he understands me.

"We need to build up a detailed profile of her," he said, like this was likely to put me off.

"That's a good idea, Matthew," I answered all wide-eyed with wonder.

He didn't say yes, he just nodded, which I take to mean go ahead.

Tuesday 6 June

LATELY I'VE BEEN reading about famous kidnappings. In some of the stories I've read, the kidnappers used chloroform to subdue their victims so I tried to find out how I could get some. I visited a chemist and started up a conversation with the pharmacist about how I'd read a book about a chloroform poisoning and was interested in how the killer could have got hold of it. He said that wouldn't have been too difficult a hundred years ago, when chloroform was used as a solvent for removing stains, but now it's been replaced by less harmful substances, so I don't think it's easily available. That's one idea out the window.

Matthew gets scared when I get specific or go into details about things, so I just keep telling him that I'm just checking things out, that

I'm not making any decisions we can't go back on. That's because he likes to believe he's the only one who can see problems and pitfalls, that a mere woman like me is likely to overlook things and needs to be kept "focused" all the time.

Men, they're all the same!

Saturday 10 June

THIS MORNING I SHOWED Matthew the dossier I've put together on Our Sarah and her father. After he'd looked it over he wanted to know if I could have alerted the librarian in any way, showing too much interest in the subject, that sort of thing.

"What kind of fool do you take me for?" I asked.

"I was just being careful," he said, not looking me in the eye.

I was so angry I had to walk away and go into the kitchen, which is something I've never done before. It was either that, or hit him over the head with a chair. Sometimes I think I've sacrificed all my principles by submitting myself to him the way I do, but it didn't start out that way. At first we were both equals, but now things have become corrupted. It's because he wants to be in charge all the time. It's his small-mindedness that's done all the damage.

Sunday 11 June

WE WENT THROUGH Matthew's question list again today. He wanted to know about specifics, he said, about how we could kidnap her, where we could keep her, etc. It was very irritating, having to listen to his lectures on "correct procedures" and so on, but I stuck it out because I think he's starting to dislike Our Sarah almost as much as I do. That's why I lay it on thick about her being "high born" and "privileged" and all the other words he doesn't like. Of course, I've still got Rod in my sights, but when I think about him now, he's taken a step back. He's standing behind Our Sarah, looking over her shoulder, grinning at me, meaning that I have to get to her first before I get to him.

We've started looking for somewhere to keep Our Sarah locked up while we negotiate for the ransom money. We need somewhere out of the way. A quiet farm or something like that out of the town is the best answer. We've also decided to ask for half a million pounds ransom. Five hundred thousand pounds. That certainly has a nice ring to it.

What I'm excited about is what started out almost as a whim now seems to be coming together like a real plan. And miracle of miracles, even Matthew's started showing a bit of enthusiasm.

I'm trying not to get too carried away because I know we've still got a long way to go.

Sunday 18 June

THIS WEEKEND WE drove out of town and spoke to a couple of estate agents. We didn't find what we were looking for, but we did see a couple of likely farmhouses and I'm sure we won't have too much trouble getting the kind of place we need. After that, it's just a case of bundling Our Sarah into a car somewhere and then waiting for the money to roll in.

Talking about money, on the way home on Saturday Matthew again said that he was thinking of packing in his job and "moving on", as he called it.

"Moving on where?" I asked.

"I don't know. Another town, I suppose."

He was hinting that he had a definite plan in mind, but I knew from the way he wouldn't look at me that it was just another of his vague schemes. The only difference this time is that he's got a bit of money behind him, which he thinks is all that matters.

I was tempted to laugh, but knew that wouldn't go down too well.

"When's this going to happen?" I asked.

I nearly said, are you expecting me to "move on" too, but I didn't think it was a good time to ask that particular question.

"Soon," he answered, like it was some kind of big secret.

I was prepared to play his silly game if that made him happy, up to a point at least, but there was one fact I had to get straight, before we went any further.

"Before or after we kidnap Our Sarah?"

His eyes shot up, like he'd suddenly realised I was on to him.

"After," he said finally.

"That's okay then," I said.

After that the conversation fizzled out, but it was disappointing to realise that I didn't feature in his plans anymore.

I think he imagines himself as some kind of great thinker, going where he wants and doing what he wants, a free and independent spirit bending the world to his will; but that's not how I see him now.

Last week, one of the girls who's just got divorced, went to see a psychologist for depression. She was asked to draw a picture of her ex-husband as she saw him now, something that would capture his character, the psychologist said.

"I drew a picture of a rat vanishing down a sewer," she said, making us all laugh.

I'd have drawn Matthew as a headless chicken running around in circles.

Up until last week, I thought he was special, but now I'm not so sure anymore. The trouble is, I need him to carry out my plan.

Sunday 9 July

I SAW OUR SARAH in the flesh for the first time on Friday afternoon. It happened quite out of the blue, which is funny because for the last few weeks I've been looking everywhere for her, but the one time I wasn't thinking about her, there she was!

I'd just come out of Tesco's with some shopping when I saw her get out of a flash sports car right across the road. Rod was behind the wheel, but he drove off before I had a chance to get a good look at him. I'm sure the car was hers because he never had that kind of money when he was going out with me. He's really landed with his arse in the butter.

I was shocked at first, seeing him there, then I felt all my old rage sweep over me. It was like a wave starting deep down under my skin. It suddenly swelled up until it filled every pore, until in the end I thought

I was going to explode with the pressure and it was only after he'd gone around a corner at the end of the street that I came to my senses again. I looked around, half expecting people to be staring at me, but no one seemed to be taking any notice. Up until that moment, I hadn't realised just how much I hated him.

I decided to follow Our Sarah for a while and I got a strange tingling sensation when I crossed the road to go after her, a kind of suppressed excitement I suppose you could call it. It was almost like seeing an old friend, someone you haven't spoken to in years. That's how I felt about her, like we were old friends, because I'd been thinking about her so much.

Following her was easy because I think she was just killing time. First, she went into a department store where she headed straight for the Women's Fashion section and spent ten minutes wandering aimlessly amongst the dresses. A couple of times she picked up one that caught her eye and held it up against her in front of a mirror, but she didn't buy anything. Then she drifted down to the cosmetic department and helped herself to a squirt of perfume at one of fragrance counters. After that she walked to the station and got a taxi.

I thought of going after her, getting into another taxi and saying, "Follow that car", but I thought it would be too dangerous and attract too much attention.

When I got home that night, I was still excited and wanted to tell Matthew what had happened, but he'd got a bee in his bonnet about how we were going to get the money if we went ahead with the kidnapping. He was also worried that Our Sarah would be able to recognise us when we let her go. I didn't say what I was thinking, that she'd likely lead the police to us no matter what we did, if we let her go, because I didn't think that would go down too well.

"We won't let that happen, Matthew," was all I said.

The look he gave me was pure incredulity.

"Really? And how are you going to work that particular miracle?"

I wanted to say, by getting rid of her, but I didn't. Instead, I said, "By staying in disguise, by keeping them blindfolded all the time and not speaking. By doing all the things you've talked about."

In other words, I appealed to his baser instinct – his ego.

"Yeah, right," he said, very offhand, but he didn't argue the point. I think he'd just had a bad day at work and wanted to share it with someone.

In the end, I never got around to telling Matthew about my brief encounter with Our Sarah. I didn't tell him that I knew Rod either. I thought it best if I kept that little secret to myself.

The good news is that yesterday we found the ideal place to hide them. It's an old shepherd's cottage about half an hour's drive out of town and miles from anywhere. The place was renovated about eighteen months ago. It's certainly in excellent condition.

We paid cash in advance for twelve months, with an option to extend the lease for a further six months if required, and everyone was very happy. Now all we have to do is get hold of Our Sarah and take her there.

Wednesday 12 July

LAST WEEK WE found out where Our Sarah's parents lived and went to look at their house, just so we knew where it was for future reference.

There was also an article in the local paper about the opening of a new nightclub called Rugs. Matthew and I are both agreed that it's just the kind of event Our Sarah's likely to go to.

We're planning to go along tonight.

Sunday 16 July

WE NOW KNOW where Our Sarah lives.

Last Wednesday, Matthew and I got dressed up and went to the opening of Rugs nightclub. I'd been looking forward to it all week, but the evening turned out to be a disappointment in the end, even though we achieved what we set out to achieve.

After a long wait to get in, Matthew, in his usual fashion, insisted on playing the wet blanket, refusing to dance or do anything that could be vaguely construed as fun because we were "at work", as he described it.

It wasn't until right at the end of the night, just when we were preparing to go home, that Our Sarah and her boyfriend turned up.

After a boring four-hour wait in the car, we followed them back to her house, watched Rod get his marching orders – she really is a bitch, that woman – then took a quick walk past her front door to make a note of the number and check out the small service road that ran around the back.

We still don't have a definite plan of action, but knowing where she lives is a very useful piece of information.

I'm surprised that Matthew still seems keen to go through with the kidnapping. I thought he was going to get cold feet sooner or later, but he seems to be almost as excited as I am about the whole thing.

Tuesday 18 July

WE'VE STARTED WATCHING Our Sarah's place from a picnic spot across the road to try and get an idea of her routine. We keep our visits random to make sure we don't create any kind of pattern. The last thing we want to do is draw attention to ourselves.

Last night we were having a picnic out of our car when the two of them came home.

He was all over her when she was trying to get her key in the door, and she was egging him on, which was disgusting to watch. That was the way Rod used to act with me after I'd let him talk me into bed. He pretended that I was special too, but all he really wanted was sex.

When I saw how she was laughing, not pushing him away, I mean, it made me really angry because she's so sure of herself, invincible almost, like nothing can touch her.

That's when I made a vow to myself that, one way or another, I was going to make her pay for taking Rod away from me.

Not long after that we packed up and went home, but we went back and drove past the house around midnight, just to see if his car was still there, which it was. Matthew also plans to go past tomorrow morning.

Everything's more or less in place now and all we have to do is carry out the kidnapping, which we have "scheduled", to use Matthew's term, for about two weeks time.

Saturday 29 July

YESTERDAY WE KIDNAPPED Our Sarah and her boyfriend. Rod was in the house when we went to get her, which was quite a shock and something we didn't expect, because we'd watched Our Sarah come home and his car wasn't parked outside, so we thought she was alone. Later on we found out he'd been inside the house all day because he'd taken his car in for a service that morning.

Anyway, we knocked on the door, pretending we wanted to use the telephone because our car had broken down, but she would have turned us away, if Matthew hadn't stuck the gun up her nose.

"Get in the house you fucking bitch," he'd said, which was quite impressive of him, I thought.

When we backed her into the house, Rod came out of the kitchen wearing an apron and for a fleeting moment I thought I was going to have a panic attack, but as soon as I realised he didn't recognise me I managed to calm down. I think it was the anger that saved me, all that lovey-dovey domestic bliss, seeing the two of them together, close up like that, I mean. It made me sick, which is why I laid into Our Sarah when I got the chance. I was so tensed up I needed to let off some steam, and she'd had it coming for a long time.

When I think back to those first twenty minutes everything's a kind of blur and there are lots of details I can't remember. It was like I was on automatic pilot: I was seeing what was going on, I was part of what was going on, but at the same time I was detached from it all, like things were happening inside a glass cage and I was on the outside.

Anyway, after we'd tied them up and put pillowcases over their heads, we got them in the car then drove out to the farmhouse.

The thing I couldn't understand was how Our Sarah had managed to get Rod eating out of her hand, like she had. Putting up with all her shit, I mean. That was all I could think about as we drove out to the farm, but it wasn't until we pulled up outside the cottage that it finally dawned on me what the attraction was: money! What man wouldn't pretend to play the devoted knight in shining armour to a pretty, empty-headed little rich girl?

There was a time when I thought Rod was special. Genuine and sincere, I mean, but now I know he's shallow and manipulative, which is something he's going to have to pay for sooner or later. That's why I get so angry sometimes when I see them together. Not because I like him any more, but because it reminds me what a fool I've been.

When Matthew turned off the engine I felt really good. That's when I turned and said, "We're home, Sarah", like we were great friends or something. It was a cruel thing to do, but I couldn't help it. She brings out the worst in me.

Matthew, as usual, was bothered by the fact that we had to change "The Plan", as he calls it, because we now had two guests and not one, but I was secretly quite happy about the whole situation. Originally, I'd thought Rod was going to have to suffer from a distance, but now he was going to be able to experience everything up close and personal, and I was going to be there to see it all happen. What could be better than that?

We put Our Sarah, who is a complete pain in the neck, in the spare bedroom and Rod went in the cellar. The good thing about Matthew is that he plans thoroughly, so we had extra chain and ropes and handcuffs and so on, so there was no problem about the pair of them being safely tied up.

After that we were able to go into the kitchen and relax for the first time since we'd knocked on Our Sarah's front door. That was when I accidentally let slip that I knew Rod's surname. It just slipped out because I was so excited and wasn't thinking straight. Needless to say, Matthew, who has a very suspicious mind, was immediately onto me, asking all sorts of questions – How do you know? What else do you know about him? etc. – but I just passed it off as something unimportant, something that I hadn't mentioned, though I'm not sure he was completely taken in. Anyway, he didn't go on about it too much, thank goodness, but it was careless of me and I know I'll have to be a lot more careful in future.

After midnight Matthew went to phone Our Sarah's parents for the first time and before he went, gave me strict instructions to stay away from our two guests, but I couldn't stop myself. No sooner was he out the door than I was down to the cellar.

190

I didn't say anything, but Rod must have known someone was there because he would have heard the door open. I think he was very tense at first, but then he seemed to relax a bit. Eventually he found his tongue.

"What do you want?" he asked, but I didn't answer, I just stood watching. He was sitting very still, but there was no sign of fear. Eventually, he said, "I haven't got any money if that's what you want," which I could have told him. I could have said, "I know everything about you. I know where you live and I know what you do," but I didn't say anything because that would have let the cat out of the bag. It's a very powerful feeling that, you knowing a lot about someone and them knowing nothing about you.

I couldn't savour the feeling though because all the time I was standing there my heart was pounding and I think my face was red, too, because I was in such a rage. I kept thinking, I used to love you. But that was a long time ago, another life almost. Now you're just a hostage, not even a real person any more.

After about a minute I turned to leave, which is when he spoke up again.

"I don't want you to hurt Sarah," he said. "She hasn't done you any harm. Let her go and keep me. Please."

Such touching concern for a fellow human being, it was all I could do not to puke.

I know I shouldn't have answered, but I couldn't help myself. I was too wound up to stay quiet, having him there in my power, I mean.

"She's the one with the money," I said.

I'd spoken in a hoarse whisper to disguise my voice and I saw him tilt his head to one side, like there was something I'd said that he couldn't quite understand. I thought he was going to say, "Sarah hasn't got any money", or "If you let us go we'll see you get paid", that sort of thing, which is why I was so shocked when he said very quietly, "Do I know you?"

That was when I felt the world lurch. I remembered too that he'd given me an odd look in the house when we'd tied him up. Now I realised that he'd been trying to look beneath my disguise, that he'd been suspicious even then.

"No," I said in the same deep put-on voice, which I knew didn't sound convincing, but he'd caught me on the wrong foot.

His chains rattled when he pushed himself up against the headboard. Then he was looking straight at me, staring at me from inside the pillowcase, which was over his head. It was like he was willing himself to see me better and even though he was blindfolded, for one frightening second I thought he knew who I was and that he was going to say something, but all he did was give a deep sigh and then the moment was gone.

I couldn't wait to get away after that, but I had a feeling of dread that it would only be a matter of time before he put two and two together. That would mean trouble if Matthew got to know, but there was another problem too. If we let Rod go sooner or later he was going to go to the police with my name. I couldn't afford to let that happen.

My heart was still beating like a trip hammer when I went into Our Sarah's room. She started moaning the instant I opened the door.

"Shut the fuck up," I said.

That made her go quiet – for a second or two anyway.

"You want to hurt me, don't you?" she whimpered.

That was the first intelligent thing she'd said all evening, but I thought it best not to say so.

"No one's going to get hurt if you both do what you're told," I lied.

"Is that a promise?" she asked.

That made me laugh. "Of course it's a promise, Sarah dear," I said sweetly. "Of course, it's a promise."

Hearing the sarcasm in my voice made her shrink back into herself.

"Leave me alone, please," she begged.

"You don't deserve to be left alone," I said, "not after the way you've treated everyone else."

She started to sob then, her whole body shaking with the effort.

"You know you make me sick, don't you, Sarah dear," I said before I walked out on her. "Sick to my stomach."

I didn't feel any pity. Not then, not ever.

I already knew that we had to get rid of Rod. But if I got rid of him then I'd have to get rid of her too.

When Matthew got back from making his phone call, he asked all sorts of questions about what I'd been up to and so on, trying to catch me out, I think. I told him that I hadn't spoken to either of them, but I'm not sure he believed me because he seems to have become very suspicious all of a sudden.

The minute Our Sarah heard him come back into the house she'd started making a noise again and I had to go and put masking tape over her mouth. I pretended to be irritated by her whining, but the real reason was because I didn't want her to tell Matthew that I'd been to see her. He just stood and watched, like I was some kind of monster, though he didn't have the balls to say so. That made me really annoyed, because at the end of the day all I was doing was taking care of business, which is something he should have done.

After that, we went down to the cellar again. That was when Rod said again that we'd get all the money we wanted, as long as no one got hurt. I think he was trying to get us into conversation, but I wasn't going to let that happen, so I bundled Matthew out as quickly as I could.

When we went to bed we were both eager to have sex. The main thing for me was to keep Matthew's mind off other things, but it turned out to be better than I expected. I think it was because we had our two guests listening to us. It made things more exciting somehow.

After that we tried to get some sleep, but without too much success, even though we'd been up for nearly twenty-four hours. At one point, I think Matthew had some kind of nightmare, because he woke up shivering and shaking, though he wouldn't say what the matter was. I just hope he's not getting cold feet all of a sudden.

At breakfast the next morning, Rod tried to talk us into letting the two of them go again. He's a cool one, I have to say that, which just goes to show how dangerous he is.

Just before lunch Matthew went to phone Our Sarah's parents again, to tell them how much money we wanted and I just stayed in the kitchen waiting for him to come back. That was because I knew that if I went to see Rod I'd end up getting into some kind of conversation, which was something I couldn't afford to do.

The minute Matthew got back he went to see Our Sarah, because he wanted to know about the ransom demand, he said. She was lying on the bed showing off her legs. She knew exactly what she was doing, trying to entice him like that, but Matthew tried to play the innocent, like he wasn't aware of what she was up to, that sort of thing. I know he fancies her, but why he can't just come out and say it, I don't know.

That was when I started going on about Rod and how dangerous he was, to take his mind off her, I mean. Out of the blue Matthew said, "You know him don't you?" taking me completely by surprise.

"Of course I don't know him!" I said, then pretended to lose my temper and walked out of the house.

Instead of dropping the subject, Matthew followed me out into the yard and kept pushing, going on about things, until in the end I told him what I thought, that we had to kill Rod. I've never seen Matthew so angry as he was then and he called me all sorts of names.

This morning Matthew went off to phone Our Sarah's parents again. He says he getting a bit of a run around from the old man, but that it's not going to be a problem. I hope he's right. This afternoon he recorded Our Sarah so that he could play her message back to her father to prove she's okay.

We also had words again. He seems to think that if we get the money and let them go then everything's going to be alright. He's living in a fool's paradise, but when I told him that he didn't want to know.

"We're going to have to kill them both," I said at one time, which made all the colour drain out of his face. I don't think he's really considered that option before.

"Give it a rest, Brenda," he said, give it a rest, like if he ignores the problem it's just going to go away.

That was the moment I knew I'd have to take matters into my own hands.

Sunday 30 July

ROD'S DEAD AND BURIED.

It happened after Matthew went to phone Our Sarah's parents tonight. After I heard him drive away, I sat in the kitchen for a long time trying to decide what to do about Rod. Eventually I went down to the cellar. I couldn't help myself, he was like a magnet, but I wasn't going to do anything, I was just going to check up on him, but that wasn't how things turned out. I only took the hammer from the garage with me for self defence.

I think he was expecting me because he was already sitting up on the bed when I walked down the steps.

"Why are you doing this, Brenda?" was the first thing he said.

One part of me knew he'd work out who I was eventually, so I shouldn't have been surprised, but I was. Suddenly, my mouth was dry and I felt my legs begin to shake. I thought of trying to bluff my way out or just stay quiet, but then I realised none of that was going to work. It was too late for subterfuge.

"How did you know it was me?" I asked.

"Your voice mainly. There was something familiar about it, even when you were trying to disguise it. And I thought I knew you when you barged into Sarah's house. It was a brilliant disguise you had on."

He was genuinely impressed. "Thank you," I said.

"But even the best disguises have their limitations."

I could tell he was pleased that he'd recognised me so quickly. Here is the Rod I know, I thought, superior and in charge. Arrogant.

"You haven't answered," he said. "Why are you doing this? You know you'll never get away with it, don't you?"

It wasn't really a question, more a statement of fact, which is why I didn't answer, not properly anyway. I still had some questions of my own.

"The money, of course," I said. I tried to sound nonchalant because I didn't want him to dwell on the real reason. "When did you work it all out?" I added.

"The final piece fell into place yesterday afternoon. I heard the two of you go outside. I think you were quarrelling. I couldn't hear what you were saying but I could hear the sound of your voice."

It was amusing to think that all the time Matthew and I were arguing about how to get away with the kidnapping, we were actually giving the game away. I suppose you could call that one of life's little ironies.

"It was also when you kicked Sarah back at the house. You got angry like that when we split up."

"We didn't split up," I said, "you split us up."

He shrugged like it was a matter of little concern.

"We'd grown tired of each other."

I hated him then. Hated him more than I've ever hated anyone. It was the way he dismissed everything, like me loving him didn't factor into the equation when he walked out. If he was an army man he'd describe me as "collateral damage", something destroyed, but only by accident and not really important.

I felt anger sweep through me like a blast of hot air. It was because he wasn't taking me seriously. He was treating the whole thing like a game, just like he had done when we were going out. I'd loved him and he used me and now he was trying to use me again.

"I hadn't grown tired of you," I said.

"It wouldn't work, Brenda. You know that. We're just too different."

What amazed me was that he wasn't even apologetic. He thought he was completely in charge – that I was going to buckle to his will.

"How come you didn't say that when you were fucking me?" I said.

"We fucked each other, Brenda," he replied, not missing a beat. Then: "So what are you going to do with us?"

"I was hurt when you dumped me," I said, avoiding the question.

"I know and I'm sorry about that, but it wouldn't have worked. We both know that."

He wasn't sorry, he was just saying that. Lying to me again.

"You didn't give it a chance," I said, playing his game.

"I didn't want to hurt you, but things would only have got worse not better. You'll thank me in the long run."

To hear him tell it, he'd done me a favour. He was the perfect gentleman who had done the honourable thing, it was me who was being unreasonable.

"Will you take the pillowcase off me?" he asked. "I need to see you if we're going to talk about this. And it doesn't serve any purpose now that I know who you are."

I pretended to give his request serious consideration. After a long pause, I said, "I will if you promise not to try anything."

"Yes, I promise."

"Okay."

"Thank you."

He was nodding, very solemn. He was so superior, like we'd just struck a formal agreement.

"Turn around," I said as I walked up to the bed, "I'm not going to do anything until I know you're still properly tied up."

"Yes, I can understand that," he replied, turning his back to me.

It was all very civilised. He was so sure of himself, he didn't have the slightest suspicion.

"Who's your partner?" he asked.

"His name's Matthew Woodgate, I said. We work together."

"And this is a bit of overtime you're putting in, is it?" he said, chuckling.

I was amazed that he could be so casual. He really did think that I was going to dance to his tune.

That was when I hit him on the head with the hammer. It was a spur of the moment thing. He just made me so furious. I lashed out without thinking. There was a dull thud, like a coconut dropped on concrete and I felt his skull give way. Suddenly there was blood running down his neck. He gave a sort of deep groan then slumped to one side, half sliding off the bed. I hit him again, once more behind the ear, but I knew he was dead. I just wanted to make doubly sure. That's when I heard Matthew pull up in the yard and I realised I was panting like a marathon runner. Everything's under control, I said to myself. Then, acting very calmly, I put down the hammer and went upstairs to meet him at the front door.

"I've killed him," I whispered, the moment Matthew stepped inside the house.

The surprising thing was that Matthew wasn't surprised, or at least he didn't act like he was. In fact, I have half a mind he was expecting it. I started to explain, making up a story about how it had happened, how

Rod had tried to attack me, how I'd had to defend myself, but he just gave me a hateful look, walked straight past and went down to the cellar, where he stood on the steps, gazing at the body. I was still tensed up and I knew I was talking too much, but I couldn't help it. Matthew didn't say anything for a long time.

"Does the girl know what you've done?" he asked.

"No."

Then he went over to take a closer look at the body, though I could see he made a point of not touching it.

"Jesus Christ!" he said.

That was when all his bitterness bubbled up. He suddenly became angrier than I'd ever seen him before. It was like a delayed reaction.

"Do you know what you've done, you idiot?" he said.

It was a stupid question, but I couldn't say that. Instead, I kept my eyes on the ground, like the wicked sinner repenting. What I really wanted was his support, but all he did was go on at me. I shall never forgive you for this, I remember thinking.

"He tried to escape," I said eventually, which started him off ranting and raving at me again. In the end I had to warn him to keep his voice down so that he didn't alert Sarah and that made him come back to his senses.

"We'll bury the body on the river bank," I said. "Tonight. After she's asleep."

Matthew didn't answer. He just walked away with his head hung forward, like he had the weight of the world resting on his shoulders.

"There's no going back, now," he said.

"There never was," I answered.

Later on I told Matthew that we had to kill the girl too. He nearly blew a fuse, which was exactly what I'd expected him to do. He went on at me about how murder wasn't part of The Plan, how it would only make things worse and so on, like The Plan, whatever that was, was inviolate. It was obvious to me though that we were in above our heads. We could hardly get rid of one victim without getting rid of the other, but I don't think he was thinking straight.

"Plans change," I said, and walked away, which made him even more angry.

Matthew didn't bring up the subject of Our Sarah again until later on.

"We have to stick to The Plan," he said, like he was trying to convince himself. "We get the ransom money, then we let her go."

"That won't work," I said. "Not now."

Matthew has never been one to take kindly to being contradicted. He stared at me, speechless, I think. If looks could kill then I'd be dead as a dodo now.

"You can't see the problem, can you?" I asked.

"What problem?"

"The problem of letting her go. If we let her go, sooner or later we'll end up in the shit."

He actually flinched when I swore, but I didn't care anymore. He needed to be shocked out of his complacency.

I nearly said: It's like you're living in a bubble, a fool's paradise, but I managed to keep my mouth shut.

"The plan is, we get the money then we let her go," he said.

That was when I saw he was trembling.

"You're the idiot if you think that's going to work," I snapped. He opened his mouth to have a go at me, but I didn't give him chance to speak. "Rod's dead," I said, "and that means he isn't a problem now. If we let her go now we're asking for trouble."

All I was doing was stating the obvious, but he wasn't having any of it.

"No," he answered, shaking his head. "If we don't let her go, we're asking for trouble!"

"You're being naive. We have to kill them both."

I've never seen him so furious as he was at that moment, homicidal almost. For a moment I was scared. I tried to be reasonable.

"Look, Matthew," I said, "once we let her go, it will only be a matter of time before the police catch up with us. Even if we move away, there's no guarantee we'll be safe."

Instead of answering, he clamped his hands over his ears, refusing to listen.

It was unreal. Here I was proposing the only possible solution and he was acting like a child making out I was the one being unreasonable.

"I'm not going to kill anyone," he said. Then he gave me a really hard stare. "You've lost control. You've gone off your head," he added.

I took a deep breath. I don't let anyone speak to me like that, and especially not when I'm the one who's thinking straight. It crossed my mind then that Matthew was becoming as big a problem as she was.

"And what happens when we go to collect the money?" I asked. "She'll be here in the house on her own. If that's not a recipe for disaster I don't know what is."

That's when he smiled. "I've thought about that, he said. We put sleeping tablets in her food."

It was so ridiculous, I couldn't believe what I was hearing, but I didn't say so. That was because I'd suddenly worked out what the problem was, why he didn't want to kill her – because he fancied her. Once that realisation dawned on me everything else just fell neatly into place.

I tried to keep my voice very matter-of-fact. "Then I hope they're extra strength," I said.

Just after midnight the two of us dragged the body out of the house. Matthew carried the shoulders, I carried the feet. We tried to be very quiet, which is difficult if you're carrying a dead body up some stairs. I was hoping we'd get out of the house unnoticed but the girl called out. "Who's there?" she said when we opened the front door. We both told her to go back to sleep.

It took us about an hour to dig a hole big enough and deep enough to bury him in. Before we covered him up I went through his pockets, but the only thing we took was the bit of cash he had on him. After that we piled the soil back and stamped it down as best we could.

By the time we'd finished, Matthew was sweating like a pig. I know he'd done most of the digging, but half of it was nerves I think.

The girl called out again when we went back into the house, but we didn't answer. We just went and had a shower then got into bed, though neither of us could sleep.

The worst thing about the whole affair is that Matthew hardly spoke to me all night. It was like he was in a sulk, blaming me for everything that had happened; yet all I'd done was take charge. I used to think he was strong, but now I know he isn't. When the chips are down, the weakling in him shines through like a lighthouse.

I saw that again outside the cottage when we stopped to take our shoes off at the front door. He kept muttering all the time and couldn't get his laces undone because his hands were shaking so much. He was so tense and I was perfectly calm and in control. It was just too obvious to miss.

That was when I realised our relationship had irrevocably changed. It was like one second we were standing next to each other and the next a huge chasm had opened up. Now the gap between us keeps getting wider all the time and sooner or later we're going to be nothing more than two tiny, isolated specs waving to each other in the distance.

I know that killing Rod wasn't something he'd expected, but that doesn't excuse everything. It doesn't excuse his head-in-the-sand mentality, for example, and it doesn't excuse the way he keeps going on at me about "sticking to The Plan" and "doing the right thing" and so on, when everything's changed. Sometimes he's so selfish I could scream.

Even thinking these thoughts makes me feel disloyal, which is why I keep putting them to the back of my mind, but I know they're not going to stay there – not forever, anyway – sooner or later they're going to spill over into the here and now – and then what happens?

Monday 31 July

THIS MORNING MATTHEW went off to work and I stayed at the farmhouse. Tonight, he reckons, we're going to see about collecting the ransom money. A "dry run" he calls it.

After he'd gone, I phoned in sick at work. I'm sure no one will think anything of it because I never take time off, but I can't keep staying away. Even if we take it in turns, sooner or later someone's going to notice that we're absent on alternative days, which could lead to trouble. What it means is we're going to have to resolve the whole thing very quickly.

I made a point of staying out of Our Sarah's way for most of the time. It was a cold day, and overcast, and I went for a walk because I couldn't settle to anything. After I'd checked the riverbank, I strolled along the lane outside the cottage. Two fields away the farmer was ploughing on his tractor. I watched him work for ten minutes then went back to the house. I didn't let him see me.

When I got back indoors Our Sarah started bleating on about being hungry so I made her some soup to eat. Then she wanted to talk, and I think she'd been crying, but I just put down the food and left without saying anything.

That was when she took to calling out for Rod. Not all the time, mind you, just occasionally, every half hour or so. When I took her a drink at lunchtime I said that we'd gagged him because he kept getting on at us, but from the look on her face I'm not sure she believed me.

"We'll do the same to you again, if you give us any more uphill," I warned.

I didn't hear a peep out of her for the rest of the day.

I can't stop keep thinking about how disappointed I am with Matthew. I know he's going to phone Our Sarah's parents again some-time today, but I just can't believe everything's going to be sorted out in the space of a weekend. And the worst is, we don't have the resources to keep anyone locked up for more than a few days, which we should have realised earlier on, I suppose. The longer she stays here, the more chance there is of something going wrong, which is another reason why we have to deal with her quickly. That's why I've decided I have to take matters into my own hands again. I have to because I can't rely on Matthew any more. It's either that or sit back and wait for the disaster to happen.

Tuesday 1 August

I KILLED OUR SARAH last night.

I didn't tell Matthew what I was planning because I knew he'd object or try to stop me, which was a complication I didn't want to deal with, things being what they are between us at present. Also, I don't trust his judgement at the moment because I think he's already halfway to having a nervous breakdown over the Rod episode, so I just knew he wouldn't have the stomach to do what was necessary. Of course, I could have killed her when he was out of the house, like I did with Rod, but this time I wanted him there as a witness and to be part of the whole thing. I wanted him involved.

This is what happened.

When Matthew got back from work, I said: "I think we need to drug the girl now, so she's asleep before we leave the farm."

He took a long time to answer, like it was a big decision and he had to weigh up a whole host of possibilities. "Yes, you're right," he said, finally, but then he went out again to phone the parents about the ransom money, so it wasn't until he got back that we actually set about getting things ready for the evening's escapade.

He used almost an entire packet of sleeping tablets, carefully mixing them in with her evening meal of vegetable soup. When the food was ready I put everything on a tray and asked him to open the door for me. That's when I picked up the big kitchen knife I'd put aside, when he wasn't looking, I mean.

"What do you want?" she asked when we walked into her room.

"We've brought you something to eat," Matthew answered.

Even though she was still blindfolded she kept her face towards the door, which is where I was standing, not looking at Matthew, who was almost next to her.

After I put the tray down on the bedside table I mumbled that I needed to check her wrists. That's when she rolled to one side, which is what I'd been expecting her to do.

"I demand to speak to Rod," she said, like she was giving an order. That was when I pulled the knife out. Out of the corner of my eye I saw Matthew lift a hand like he was about to stop me and I remember the look of horror on his face, but by then it was already too late. That was when everything slipped suddenly into slow motion.

I meant to stab her in the throat, but she must have sensed the movement because she twisted away even in the instant the knife was coming down, so it struck her in the shoulder, went into the flesh, making the blood spurt. She screamed and lashed out, kicking me in the side, but I didn't feel the blow, it was only later when I was in the shower that I saw the big purple bruise just above my hip bone, but I didn't stop, I just kept stabbing and stabbing, feeling the knife cut into muscle and bone. Then just as suddenly as she'd started fighting and shouting she went limp and it was all over.

I looked up. Everywhere was covered with blood and there was Matthew with his mouth open, staring at me like a dumbstruck fool. I was so angry then, I could have killed him too.

"A lot of good you were," I said and wiped the knife on the sleeve of her dress. Then I unlocked the girl's handcuffs.

I think Matthew had gone into a state of shock because he didn't move. He just watched me.

I was all for leaving her there until we got back from town, but he wouldn't hear of it.

"We can't leave her here," he said, all wide-eyed and hysterical, so I said, "OK, if that's what you want," and went and got a bowl of cold water. I was taking charge. I had to. He was incapable. After that we got down to cleaning up the room, which we did in silence.

The weird thing is I'd expected him to go on at me, but he didn't say a word, although one time I did catch him staring at me, giving me a really funny look, like he was looking at some kind of nasty insect he'd never seen before.

Before we left the house we wrapped Our Sarah's body in plastic bags and dragged her out of the back door and into the bushes. When that job was done, I changed clothes to drive into town because the ones I had on were covered with blood.

"It's just a bit of blood," Matthew, I said, when I caught him looking at me undressing in the kitchen, but he didn't seem to think it was funny. I didn't expect him to be so squeamish about the blood.

When I told him that we had to go and get the money, he just nodded and walked outside and got in the car.

After that we went off and did our "dry run" as he called it, but it was like being out with a zombie.

Fortunately everything went very smoothly. The old man did exactly what he was told and neither of us saw anything out of the ordinary, although I don't think Matthew would have noticed anything suspicious anyway, given the state he was in.

When we got back to the farm we buried Our Sarah next to her boyfriend, working in the pouring rain with next to nothing on until nearly two o'clock in the morning. It was my idea to take our clothes off. It wasn't because there would be fewer clues that way, but because

I knew we were going to end up covered in mud again and didn't want to have to throw away any more things. "Thank goodness it's summer," I said to Matthew, but I don't think he appreciated the joke.

Wednesday 2 August

WE GOT THE MONEY last night – five hundred thousand pounds! No trouble, no fuss, except that Matthew had wanted to chicken out, but I wouldn't let him. All of a sudden he's got cold feet. It's as if he imagines that killing the girl but then not collecting the ransom will somehow make everything all right.

I dressed up for the event. The same disguise I used for the kidnapping. When I stopped Our Sarah's old man after we'd had him running around for an hour, he didn't seem to realise what was happening and he was clutching the bag so tightly to his chest I almost had to break his arm to get at it.

"Where's Sarah?" he asked, when I began to walk off again.

"She'll be free by the time you get home," I replied. "Just wait for her call."

He started to come after me, but I waved him away.

"Don't try to follow me."

The last thing I saw was him standing on the pavement, white-faced and trembling, not knowing what to do.

I expected Matthew to come out of his depression and show some excitement when he saw the money, but he wasn't interested.

"Is it all there?" he asked.

"Yes, of course," I said, trying to sound enthusiastic, but it didn't make any difference.

After that we drove back to his flat in silence and the next time he spoke was when we were pulling up in the street.

"Now what?" he said.

"Now we count the money."

"We've got to get our priorities right," he said.

He wasn't talking about the money; he was talking about me. What he meant was, I've got to get *my* priorities right, as if I was the problem and he was the solution.

Matthew had another little surprise for me yesterday – he's handed in his notice in at work. I can't say I'm surprised, but I'm disappointed that he didn't discuss it with me beforehand. I didn't go on at him, which I know is what he expected me to do, because it's too late for recriminations.

Wednesday 9 August

MATTHEW AND I ARE FINISHED. History. Kaput. All over bar the shouting. We both know it but neither of us has said anything.

I can't stand the way he looks at me, the tone of his voice, the way he pulls away when I go to touch him. I think I first noticed the change in him at the farmhouse after we'd buried Rod. He became detached then he seemed to lose interest in everything. He wasn't interested in me, he wasn't interested in the money, he wasn't interested in anything – except himself, of course.

The Matthew mantra I call it: me, me, me.

And after Our Sarah everything just got worse. Nowadays he just mopes around at work and in the evenings he doesn't want to do anything but sit around in his flat all the time. And when I ask him what he's going to do after he leaves Thompsons, he just shrugs, as if it's none of my business. That's why I've been forced to come up with a scheme to protect myself. Plan A, I call it, because I'm afraid he's going to do something stupid and get us both into trouble.

This morning I began to put Plan A into effect – I went to see Mrs Williams.

"My Aunt Mary's very sick, Mrs Williams," I said, after she'd invited me to sit down.

That, by the way, was a surprise, her asking me to sit down, I mean, then she suddenly looked full of concern, which was something else I hadn't expected.

After a pause she said, "I'm very sorry to hear that, Brenda. Are the two of you very close?"

"She brought me up, Mrs Williams," I said.

When I went on to explain how my aunt's condition had suddenly deteriorated, how she needed someone to look after her, she became quite emotional. That's when she reached out and squeezed my hand across the desk.

"My mother's very sick too," she said, starting to choke up.

When I said that I was worried about my job and maybe having to take time off work, her eyes filled up with trembling tears and she shook her head, like that wasn't important.

"You just take as much time as you need," she said. "You hear me, Brenda? You take all the time you need."

"Thank you for being so understanding, Mrs Williams," I said, when I got up to leave ten minutes later.

By that time she was already fishing in her handbag for a handkerchief.

"I know how horrible it can be when someone you love is poorly," she whispered, dabbing at her eyes.

Walking back to my desk I was elated because I couldn't believe my luck that the meeting had gone so well.

When I told Matthew the lie about Aunt Mary, his reaction was just the opposite of Mrs Williams's: he didn't show even the slightest sympathy. "I'm sorry to hear that, Brenda," he said, but he was just saying that, a blind man on a galloping horse could see he didn't mean it.

The saddest thing is that things have finally come to this. Everything started out fine, but these days I'm not even sure we have a relationship any more. Now he thinks I'm just another "stupid female". A liability. A millstone around his neck. He hasn't said so, but I know that's what he's thinking. That's why I have to protect my own interests – because Matthew won't.

When I said that we needed to go back to the farmhouse this weekend, he was dead against the idea, I could tell that from his expression.

"I don't want to go back either, Matthew," I said, pretending to be as uncomfortable about the whole thing as he was, "but we have to keep up appearances. It can't be helped."

He muttered something about never wanting to see the place again.

"We need to make sure there's no incriminating evidence lying about," I said. "We have to act like nothing out of the ordinary has happened."

That was when he pulled a face. He didn't say anything, but I know he was thinking about the two bodies buried in the ground next to the river.

"It would be silly to get caught just because we didn't see things through to the end," I said. "We have to act naturally."

He gave me such a cool look it was almost scary, then a second later he was grinning like a madman.

"Maybe we should have a painting weekend," he giggled. "Maybe we should paint out Our Sarah's bedroom? You know, to get rid of all those unpleasant memories?"

He wasn't trying to be constructive he was being hurtful.

"We don't have a choice," I said.

I thought he was going to argue the point, but his mood changed again. He just shrugged and didn't say anything.

"I think we should drive out on Friday night," I said.

I took it to mean okay when he didn't answer.

Thursday 10 August

AFTER WORK YESTERDAY I bought a pair of earrings because I needed something to make myself feel better. When Matthew saw them he went crazy, going on at me about spending the money we'd stolen, drawing attention to ourselves, etc. etc. etc.

"They're just a pair of earrings, Matthew," I said, but he didn't want to listen. He made me mad and I argued with him because I felt like a volcano getting ready to explode, but it made no difference. He wouldn't listen because I'd committed the cardinal sin: I'd broken the first Commandment of Matthew: I am thy Lord and Master. Thou shall have no other before me.

It was while he was ranting and raving that I suddenly realised what it is that I don't like about him: he doesn't get pleasure like a normal person, seeing someone else have a good time. He's only happy when he's in complete control and making that person's life a misery, which is a very unhealthy personality trait, in my opinion.

Who does he think he is?

Sunday 13 August

IT'S FINALLY OVER. Finished. The end.

Friday was Matthew's last day at work and I organised a small leaving party for him. No one was very interested, because he was so unpopular, but I said that we couldn't let him leave without making some kind of effort, which most people agreed with in the end, after I'd twisted their arms a bit. I also organised a whip round to raise some money, but not everyone had contributed so the firm had to chip in £5 to make up enough money to buy him a gold-plated pen and pencil set.

At lunchtime, when we were having our little party outside his office, Mrs Williams gave a short speech, wishing him well and giving him the gift, which he accepted with good grace, although he was very embarrassed to be the centre of so much attention.

Someone asked him what he was planning to do and he said that he hadn't made up his mind yet, but that he was thinking of moving away. He didn't mention that he hasn't talked to me about his plans for the future.

After work we drove out to the farm together. Matthew hardly said a word during the entire journey. Even though it was a beautiful warm summer's evening – the sun slanting through the trees, the birds chirping, etc. – he was in one of his moods. Giving me the silent treatment, I called it.

"What's wrong with you?" I asked when we pulled up outside the farmhouse.

"Nothing," he answered.

"Then why are you acting so miserable?"

At first I didn't think he was going to reply, then after a long pause he said, "We've killed two people," like that explained everything.

"So?" I said.

The look he gave me was incredulous. "What do you mean, so? Killing anyone wasn't part of the plan."

"We didn't have a choice, Matthew," I said, but I could tell from the look on his face that he wasn't convinced.

"I saved our lives," I said.

That was when he laughed at me.

"You're off your head, you know that, don't you?" he said.

I was about to answer, but he didn't give me a chance. He went over to the riverbank, where he wandered around for ten minutes, leaving me to unpack the car. That's when I found the golf club in the boot.

Don't tell me he's taking up golf because he thinks he's moved up in the world, I remember thinking, then all of a sudden the hair on the back of my neck stood up on end. It was a very unpleasant sensation – believe me, like an alarm bell going off. That's when it first struck me that I needed to be more cautious, that Matthew might have a Plan A of his own that he wasn't telling me about, though what made me think like that I'm not really sure.

Our landlord chose to pay us a visit just as I was carrying the last bag inside and Matthew was walking back to the cottage. I glanced over at him as he emerged from the trees: there was panic written all over his face in big, bold letters.

"Just stay calm," I said to him.

The farmer pulled up outside the front door, but didn't get out of his Landrover.

"I saw you drive up, he said. I thought I'd pop over and see that everything's alright."

"Everything's perfectly fine, thank you," I said.

"And you, Mr Woodgate? No complaints, I hope?"

Matthew just stood there with a stupid grin on his face, looking guilty.

"Everything's fine," he managed to say.

The farmer gave him a puzzled look, but didn't say anything.

"Perhaps you'd like to come in for a cup of tea," I said.

"No, thank you. I just wanted to make sure there were no problems."

"It's really no trouble," I persisted. I was trying to distract him because he was staring at Matthew again.

That was when he smiled at me. It was like a spell breaking.

"Next time, maybe," he said, engaging a gear.

I waved him off as he headed back down towards the road, but I was fuming because I realised just how close Matthew had come to breaking point. I knew that all it would take was a loose word or gesture for the floodgates to open and for the world to come tumbling down around our heads.

The minute the farmer had gone I rounded on him. I couldn't help it.

"If you don't pull yourself together you're going to get us into big shit," I shouted before I marched back into the house, but he didn't answer.

We were sitting in the kitchen half an hour later when Matthew said: "I don't think we can go on seeing each other any longer."

I wasn't surprised because I knew it was coming. I'd been expecting it for days. In true Matthew fashion he was blaming me for everything that happened. He wasn't blaming himself. The responsibility was all mine. That's when I snapped.

"Is that what you think?" I said.

"Yes."

I was standing at the sink, preparing supper; he was sitting at the kitchen table. I turned to look at him, but he looked away, because he couldn't face me. That's when I lost it.

I picked up the frying pan, spun round with it and struck him as hard as I could flat in the face. It was heavy, made out of cast iron and I felt his nose split, spraying blood all over the table, then he slid sideways off his chair, in a daze. I hit him again on the top of the head, breaking the handle clean off in the process, and after that he went down like a ton of bricks. Then I dumped some of the groceries we'd brought with us out on the floor and put the plastic bag over his head, squeezing it tight around his neck until he stopped breathing. He didn't even put up a struggle.

When I knew he was dead, I dragged his body next to the door and switched out the lights. Then I had to go and lean against the table to give my heart a chance to stop pounding.

I hadn't planned for things to go like that. What I was intending to do was drug his food then use a pillow on him from out of the bedroom, but the end result was the same, so I don't suppose it matters too much.

When I'd calmed down enough to think clearly, I cleaned up the mess in the kitchen, then wrapped his body in some big plastic bags and waited for it to get dark. After midnight, I dragged his body out to the riverbank.

Digging a hole big enough to put him in took me nearly three hours and working in the dark was kind of spooky, knowing that there were two other dead bodies decomposing not far away, I mean. Of course, I considered putting Matthew in with Rod and Our Sarah but then decided not to, mainly because to bury him I'd have to uncover them, which was something I didn't fancy doing.

After that, I went back to the house and tried to sleep, but the place creaked too much so in the end I just lay tossing and turning until it got light. The next day I stayed around the farm all the time. I wanted to check the gravesite in the daylight to make sure I hadn't left any telltale signs that would give the game away and this afternoon I covered the area with some leaves and twigs and was pretty satisfied with my handiwork.

Monday 14 August

I DROVE BACK TO town this morning and then phoned Mrs Williams to say I needed a day off to take care of some things for my sick aunt. After that I went around to Matthew's flat and collected the holdall containing the money we had stored there. Then I phoned his landlord to say he'd had to go away to visit his sick mother in France and wouldn't be back. (I included the France bit because I thought it sounded more serious somehow.) Of course, the landlord was very upset, but when I said that Matthew had left three months rent to allow for all the inconvenience that seemed to put him in a much happier frame of mind, all the more so because Matthew's contract only stipulated that he give one month's notice. I was very apologetic and said that Matthew had asked me to arrange to have his furniture removed.

After that I went to a removal firm and got them to strip the flat for me, saying that the resident had moved away suddenly. I got them to take all his furniture, which wasn't a lot, to the local hospice.

In the afternoon I went to the bank, where I spoke to Mr Royston, the assistant manager, about getting a safety-deposit box. I'd decided that I didn't want all that money lying about the flat where someone could stumble over it and ask all sorts of embarrassing questions, but I couldn't just deposit it in my bank account either, so a safety-deposit box seemed like the perfect solution.

Mr Royston was very helpful. I pretended to be the innocent, helpless female, of course, which always brings out the best in a man. He showed me what forms to fill out and even got some of the deposit boxes out of the storeroom so that I could see the different sizes. I took the largest, of course.

I also got a phone call from the matron at the hospice saying how grateful she was for the donation I'd made, which was very nice of her, I thought.

Tuesday 15 August

I WENT BACK TO WORK TODAY. Everyone was very sympathetic when I said that my aunt's condition hadn't changed and that I might have to go and look after her full time if she got any worse. I told them that because I need to keep my options open, I haven't decided whether or not I'm going to stay at Thompsons. I'm even toying with the idea of going abroad, Greece or Italy possibly, but I haven't made my mind up about that yet.

I took the safety-deposit box back to the bank at lunchtime. Mr Royston – he said that I should call him Stephen – helped me with the formalities again. He was very attentive, opening doors for me, and so on and later phoned me at work and asked me if I'd care to go out with him. I said yes without the slightest hesitation.

I realise that a professional person in his position is expected to be polite and know how to conduct himself properly, but I could tell straight away that there was some kind of special bond between us.

I know I once said the same kind of thing about Matthew and matters didn't work out as well as they should have done, but circumstances were completely different then, me being so vulnerable when we first met and him taking advantage of me, I mean. This time I shall be a lot more careful and restrained, not throwing caution to the wind and letting my heart rule my head like I did the last time.

This morning there was an article in the newspaper about Sarah Fitzgibbon and her boyfriend going missing. The police suspect they've been kidnapped, the article claimed. There was some speculation that the IRA was involved. There was also a picture of her father, who begged the kidnappers to return his daughter and her boyfriend as soon as possible.

I don't think there's much chance of that happening, to be truthful.

Sunday 3 September

IT'S BEEN A VERY BUSY MONTH.

Last week I finally handed in my notice at work. I said that I have to go and look after my aunt who has become sick again. I also gave my flatmate a month's notice and I've bought myself a flat. I used a little bit of money from the wages job as a deposit and I've taken out a mortgage for the rest, even though I could pay for the place twice over if I wanted to. That's because I don't want anyone asking questions about how I've become rich all of a sudden.

The flat is in a very good part of town, by the way, and not far away from where Our Sarah used to live. It has two bedrooms, a modern kitchen, a large lounge and a lovely balcony that looks down onto the river.

Stephen has been very helpful, speaking to the lawyers about the transfer and setting up the insurance and so on.

He took me out for a meal and then to the cinema on our first date, and we've become very close since then. These days he sleeps over at my place quite often.

He's much more considerate than Matthew and being properly educated and in the world of finance, he's very concerned about practical money matters, so I'm getting very good advice, though I haven't told him how much money I've got or anything like that.

We spent last weekend at the farm and had a lovely time. On the Sunday morning we even had a stroll along the riverbank, quite near to where Matthew and the others are resting, not that anyone would notice now that a few weeks have passed. (I've been back a couple of times since

Matthew and I were last there. I've repainted the bedroom Our Sarah was in and put down a large carpet in the cellar over the spot where there's a red stain on the concrete.) I haven't told Stephen about Matthew, of course, because he gets jealous sometimes and he has a short temper and can say hurtful things, though he always apologises later on, after he's cooled down, I mean. All I've told him is that I rented the farm out because I like to get away from things at the weekend, using some money my father left me in his will.

Even though I know Stephen has "an eye for the ladies" as my mum used to call it, I'm positive he won't disappoint me like all the others did. He calls me his Special Girl, for one thing, and he's very considerate, always calling me when one of his business meetings runs late into the night, and so on. That's why I'd be devastated if I found out he'd been unfaithful or anything like that, because it's happened to me before, so I know how much it hurts.

Like when P talked me into going for a walk in the woods with him that time. Eighteen months ago that was, though I can still remember what happened as clear as if it was yesterday.

All he really wanted me for was sex and after that he didn't care.

It was after he'd zipped himself up, after he'd told me that I shouldn't take things so seriously, that I finally snapped. I couldn't help myself.

There was a piece of a tree branch on the ground, which I picked up almost without thinking when he turned to walk away from me. The first time I hit him, the wood split from end to end, but it brought him to his knees. The second blow laid him out flat. I hit him a third time when he was lying on the ground, still twitching. After that he never moved again.

I hid his body, then drove his car back into town and parked it in a multi-storey car park near where he worked. When it was dark that night, I went back to the woods and buried his body. Not long after that, I moved up north and got a job at Thompsons. And the rest, as they say, is history.

I know a lot of girls can forgive their man anything, but I'm not like that because I won't let myself be taken advantage of. And everything's perfect now, which is why I'd be so upset if I heard anything horrible about Stephen.

To be honest, if that happened I really don't know what I'd do.